CURSES, DIAMONDS, & TOADS

A Fairy Tale Retelling

Amy Trent

Grace Burrowes Publishing

Curses, Diamonds, & Toads

Copyright © 2024 by Amy Trent

All rights reserved.

No part of this book may be reproduced in any form or by any electronic or mechanical means, including information storage and retrieval systems, without written permission from the author, except for the use of brief quotations in a book review.

This book may not be used to prompt, train, or otherwise interact with any generative artificial intelligence model whatsoever.

Curses, Diamonds, & Toads is a work of fiction. Any resemblance to reality is coincidental.

To My Sister, Ona
I love you.

CHAPTER ONE

Speaking was a hard habit to break, even with an abundance of motivation. It took me three years and seven villages before I learned to school my tongue. Market days made me sweat before I was sure I had mastered my silence. The fear that impulse or habit would cause me to slip back into words made me nervous for days. Now, I sat in the alley in my tattered gray hood with my baskets of wares, preoccupied only with my empty purse and empty stomach.

"A new peddler?" a passing lady whispered to her gentleman. She giggled before addressing me. "Or are you yet another nameless wench trudged up from the coast to ruin our fair town?" She bumped one of my baskets with a careless step.

I steadied the basket, my skin prickling at the thought of it toppling over.

"Well?" the lady demanded, adjusting her parasol.

Of course I was from the coast. My sun-kissed skin and dark hair made that fact apparent, but I was hardly nameless.

Astrid Lucia. Astrid Lucia. My name rattled in my head, tempting my tongue, but my stomach knew better. It twisted and writhed as I recalled the shrieks of disgust that ensued whenever I spoke. Being nameless and speechless was a small price to pay if it meant not being run out of another village.

My tongue remained pressed to the roof of my mouth. My lips would not part, but apparently the lady was dumber than the lace parasol she twirled about. So I shook my head and tapped the front of my neck with my hand.

"I think she's mute, dearest," the gentleman said. He dropped a single halfpenny in the dust at my feet. "Come now. Much more to see in the square." He offered his arm to the lady, who smiled, swung her parasol to her other shoulder, and flounced away, kicking up an abundance of dust as I stooped for the halfpenny.

Business would have been better in the bustle of the cobbled square, but I didn't want to risk a fuss. Word would spread soon enough—all it would take was one curious child. I swatted my cloak clean and adjusted my skirts, being careful to shake them free of dust, before I dozed against the cool plaster wall behind me. I stirred only when I heard the clink of coins. I never heard many. Shrieks and gasps, on the other hand, were common. As were the boys who laughed and jeered when an unsuspecting villager lifted one of the lids of my baskets. Most didn't take kindly to the shock of my wares.

Larger footfalls and deeper voices approached.

"A surprise?" The tanner was being dragged by his son down the alley. "Am I to guess?"

"Yes!" The boy was all giddiness. He'd come earlier and peeked inside my baskets when he thought I dozed.

"Strudels and tarts, is it?" The tanner caught his son and tossed him in the air. "Tin soldiers?"

"No!" The boy laughed.

The tanner saw my baskets, his smile still fixed on his face. "Surely not pups and kittens again."

"Better!"

"Dragon's teeth and unicorn hair?" He lifted the lid of my largest basket and yelped before laughing loud and long. "Snakes?"

"And lizards and toads!" the boy said with earnest delight. "May I have one?"

"What? Pay for vermin?"

I bristled. If I could have spoken, I would have told the tanner that the black snake ate vermin, hunting mice and rats that plagued barns like his. The spotted toad would gobble up the flies that vexed his sows. The lizards would make quick work of the slugs on his squash vines.

"I'm not parting with coin for beasties you should be digging out of the garden. Come along. We can't waste time on market day."

By dusk, I'd earned only a couple of halfpennies and the assurance that I'd be digging forest roots for supper for another week. I was tying up my baskets when the potter found me. Easy enough to spot potters. Clay clung to them, even when they scrubbed up for market, just as tannins stuck to tanners. Clay smelled so much nicer than leather, though. Not as nice as flour, and most assuredly not as nice as sugar, but clay and the men who worked with it still had a sweet earthiness about them.

Once upon a time, before I crossed the vile fairy, I used to daydream about the type of man I might marry. While potters were not at the top of my list, the way bakers, merchants, even millers were, they definitely merited my consideration.

It was with some of that lost fondness that I appraised, perhaps too generously, the man approaching me. Narrow but strong shoulders. Tall with no paunch protruding at his middle. No streaks of gray in his windblown blond hair either.

"Thank heavens you're still here." He jogged a step closer. He was a young man, probably only a handful of years older than me, but even so, creases were forming at the corners of his blue eyes. His unruly beard was flecked with gray. "I was worried I missed you."

I frowned. No one ever missed me.

"May I?" He gestured to my baskets.

My brow furrowed, but I nodded, marking how his deft, competent hands made quick work of the knots I'd tied. He lifted a lid, his eyes growing wide like a bullfrog's, before a grin broke across his face.

My stomach turned, not out of fear and certainly not out of disgust. The potter was a handsome man when he smiled, even with an unkempt beard.

"These are exceptional," the potter said, sifting through the basket. He pointed to the pink-and-white-striped snake. "Is that a corn snake?"

I nodded.

"I've never seen the like." He continued to inspect my baskets of toads and snakes, skinks and salamanders, lizards and frogs. His hands, though not caked in clay, still bore mud under the fingernails. "May I?" He gestured to one of the small ribbon snakes.

I kept my lips sealed tight, but allowed the request.

He picked up the snake gently, without even a hint of a grimace or shiver of suppressed revulsion. "Remarkable." He stretched the snake out long before coiling it and returning it to the basket. "How much?"

I held up a single finger then pinched my forefinger and thumb together.

"A halfpenny?" The potter laughed. "Forgive me. I meant how much for these baskets?"

All of my baskets? I nearly gasped, but three years of being run out of towns had well schooled me to remain silent. I held up two fingers before touching my ring finger to my thumb.

"Four silver crowns?"

I nodded. It would be enough coin for me to buy bread for a month and then some. It might even be enough for me to buy a wheel of cheese. It'd certainly be the first streak of good fortune I'd had since the curse began.

His purse rattled as he counted out the coins. "A hard but fair bargain." He dropped the coins directly into my hand. "Do you think you could find more?"

I smiled. Of course I could *find* more.

"Excellent. My house is at the top of the hill, past the meadow. Can't miss it."

CHAPTER TWO

The next week, I trudged up the steep hillside with new baskets full of my creatures.

The potter opened his door in bare feet. "Hello again." He was completely covered in mud. His smile was still handsome, though. "Do come in," he said, ushering me inside his home.

It was a well-appointed house, with plaster walls, glass windows, and wood floors. I wasn't surprised by the tracks of mud in the hallway—it had been a very wet spring—but I was shocked by the state of his front room. This room that faced the road, and should have been the prettiest in the house, was the potter's studio. His potter's wheel sat in one corner, while tables of supplies and tools cluttered the center of the room. Shelves of finished pieces lined the opposite wall. There was nowhere to sit, save at the wheel, not that I'd want to. The room was absolutely filthy.

"I'm Bernard, by the way."

Bernard. The name suited the potter. I curtsied but said nothing.

"My mother would have boxed my ears for not introducing myself at the market the other day."

She should have boxed his ears for the state of the studio. I'd never seen so much mud indoors.

"She'd offer you tea if she were here. She's not." He cleared a space on one of his tables for my baskets. "Hasn't been for years. It's just me, I'm afraid."

Bernard rubbed his mud-covered hands on his front. I winced when I realized he wasn't wearing a work apron. It'd take hours, if not days, to get the clay out of his clothes. The linen might wear through in the process.

"Let's see what you've got." He surveyed my baskets, letting the odd word of amusement fall from his lips. He stole a glance at me, which was peculiar, as I made no pretense of hiding my study of him. "I bet you're wondering what a potter is doing collecting reptiles and amphibians."

I shrugged. Truthfully, I was wondering what a potter was doing barefoot in his studio. Perhaps his mother had scolded him often enough in his youth about ruining his boots with mud that he'd given up wearing them at home altogether.

It would be nice to know. It'd be nicer still to ask. There was a facility to conversation that I'd never appreciated when words had come without consequence. How easy it had been to tease and encourage, thrust and parry. To say exactly what you thought and not give up asking until you had an answer.

But my curse had resigned me to acceptance about not only my fate but the fate of my wares. Some people collected creatures. Some people ate them. Others used them for what nature intended—to hunt prey. Occasionally, a man of learning bought one for scientific study. I suspected that was a pretense for torture or perhaps collecting venom for an equally dark purpose. What did I care as long as I had coin for bread?

Bernard rubbed his beard with a single knuckle. "I could attempt to explain, but it'd be faster to show you."

I made a sweeping gesture. *By all means.*

His blue eyes twinkled as he dipped a small viper in a murky jar of liquid on his worktable before coiling it on a tablet of wet clay. "It took me several attempts. I ran through all of the specimens I purchased from you at market, but I have"—Bernard adjusted the creature's head—"at last perfected my technique. Now..." His voice pitched higher as he addressed the snake. "Don't move, and you will be immortalized. Move, and you die for nothing." He worked quickly, packing wet plaster around the animal. "I take a cast, and then I can make an exact likeness in clay. The plaster captures every last detail."

I looked on, my gaze cool, my lips shut in a firm line.

"Don't be like that," the potter chided. "The creature was going to die either way. Now, our little friend will adorn some grand duchess's table." He wiped his hands on his shirt. Again. "Look." He'd retrieved a plate from the top of one of his shelves. "It's not fired yet. The colors will be brighter when it is."

The platter he handed me was adorned with clay toads and lizards, exact replicas of the living animals. Even in the muted rusts and grays, it was breathtaking.

"All the fine ladies will marvel at the beauty that is perfectly preserved in the ceramic. And then"—Bernard pressed a finger into the wet plaster of his latest cast on the table—"they will pay me handsomely for their own earthenware, which reminds me."

He reached into his pocket and rattled out a couple of silver coins.

"I'll take the lot," he said, gesturing to my baskets. "But I'll need more. I want small. Pretty. These fellows here are too fat." He held up a warty toad and pulled out a large bull snake. "But they'll be helpful additions to my garden."

I pushed the coins back at the potter.

"You don't want the work?" His voice grew quiet, confused. "You disapprove of my method?"

I stared at him, catching his eyes and smiling. I had no love lost for the creatures.

He added an extra copper coin to the pile and then another. I swept the money into my purse.

"Come back after market day, if you've found anything," Bernard said.

He returned to his wheel, leaving me to show myself out.

I didn't go to market that week. I was too busy collecting the smallest and prettiest of my specimens for Bernard.

When I returned to the potter's house, my baskets were full of small toads and frogs, delicate-looking lizards, and snakes so small they could be confused for worms. The potter saw me from his mud-splattered windows and greeted me at the door before I could knock. His smile made me glad I had combed and braided my hair.

The potter rubbed his eye, leaving behind bits of plaster in his blond lashes. He grimaced when he looked inside my baskets. "Like writhing noodles. Enough to make your stomach turn."

I blushed at that. I didn't care that the poor creatures were doomed if it meant more coin in my purse, but I hated that my fate was so irrevocably connected with theirs.

He sighed, looking at the growing assortment of ceramic pieces on his shelves. "I'll take the lot." He handed me a gold sovereign. "But no more skinny ones. The ladies hate anything that reminds them of those among us who are underfed. Not that they are interested in doing anything about it."

I bit my lip to keep from smiling.

"I suppose I should not say such things." Bernard bent his head conspiratorially. "Criticizing the clientele is not comely."

Even if such criticism was well deserved? I arched an eyebrow and tilted my chin up to meet his gaze.

Bernard paused with slightly parted lips before straightening. "I must get back to work. Until next week."

At market that week, I bought a new cloak and a pair of pale blue hair ribbons. No one cared that I could only point and gesture. My coin did all the necessary talking.

My breath came in shallow huffs when I knocked on Bernard's door the following day.

The potter stared at me, bleary-eyed, in the morning sunshine. "You again?"

My smile tightened. Had Bernard seen through my pretty ribbons and cloak? He was bound to tire of me eventually, but I had hoped to read the signs before I sank to the level of my wares—unwanted vermin, nauseating pests.

I sighed. I'd been called much worse. Better to know what this was about now and be done with it.

He left his door open even after I stepped inside with my basket.

"I can't pay you. I haven't sold any of the other pieces yet. No sales means no money." He shuffled, barefoot, back to his wheel.

No name-calling. No demand to get out of his sight.

My brow furrowed as I surveyed his cluttered studio. Stacks of glossy and colorful earthenware were piled haphazardly on his shelves, along with several fine and finished, unadorned pieces. Large lumps of gray clay cluttered the floor around Bernard's wheel, which was still turning. His worktables were just as cluttered as I remembered them, and all of his tools showed signs of proper and frequent use.

The man appeared tired, yes, but not ill. His hands moved deftly, calling forms and shapes out of the cone of clay turning on his wheel, so strong drink was not the reason he was bleary-eyed.

I approached Bernard and placed a single hand on my hip. *What happened?*

"My washwoman left me... Said what I was doing was unnatural. Also..." He quickly dipped his hands in the basin of water at his side and reapplied them to his clay. Muddy water splattered everywhere. "She said she'd be damned if she ever scrubbed mud off one more of my shirts. I can't take my commissions to the fine houses in town until I get"—he fingered the crusted clay on the front of his vest—"sorted."

I rolled up my sleeves and noticed how Bernard's eyes drifted from the clay on his wheel to my slender wrists. About time.

I grabbed an apron that hung idly on a peg on the wall.

Bernard smoothed his untidy beard. "You want to be my washwoman?"

I narrowed an eye and held up two fingers before touching my middle finger to my thumb.

"Two pence a week? Is that all? Gracious, do you cook as well?"

My lips curled into a smile.

"Right, I'm getting ahead of myself. Upstairs." He gestured to the stairs across the hall from his studio. "The washbasin and pump are out back." He rose and rummaged through a small cupboard before pressing a mud-streaked pail into my hand. "The lye, or whatever else is used to make it come clean—the chickens were getting curious, so I had to bring it inside." His touch was soft, gentle, in spite of the clay crusted on his hands. He stepped back. "Stay clear of the kiln."

I kept my hovel in the woods cleaner than Bernard did his home, and his upstairs rooms were as filthy as his studio. Cobwebs and trails of ants. Mud smeared on every surface. Piles of dirty clothes that looked worse than my old tattered cloak ever had. Crumbs and half-eaten food left on dirty plates that filled the tables and overflowed onto the floors. The linens hadn't been properly washed in weeks, and the rooms surely hadn't known a cross breeze for months. His basin and pitcher for ablutions were filled with muddy water.

And people recoiled at my tidy baskets of creatures. No wonder his washwoman had quit.

I unlatched and opened every last window. I stripped his bed, unfastened the curtains, and tossed them all down the stairs. I threw his clothes down next.

Bernard was the only reason I had bread to eat, a comb for my hair, and the comfort of pennies saved in my purse. Before him, I'd spent every day, apart from market day, foraging in the woods. Never mind that I was fond of his deep voice, bright eyes, and honest grin—Bernard was my golden goose, and gracious, he deserved some cosseting.

I worked quietly, though I felt like screaming at the man on several occasions that day. Like when I saw that his vegetable garden had not been harvested for weeks. Who would let a squash grow to the size of a footstool?

There was so much mud. I boiled, scrubbed, and wrung his work clothes five times over, his sheets and quilts at least thrice. It was as if the man had rolled his bed linens in the muddy banks of the creek.

I showed Bernard my work as the sun set, leading him to his newly clean, freshly filled basin and pointedly indicating he should wash his hands before I would allow him to touch the still-drying clean clothes. His linens and curtains were back in place. And his bedchamber, at least, had been cleaned and scrubbed of all crumbs and dirt.

"It smells so sweet." He fell onto his bed, not bothering to do anything about his soiled clothes, and I cringed.

I brought him the finer clothes that I had painstakingly washed and pressed dry.

"They do look nice," he said.

I showed him the ripped cuff of his shirt and pantomimed a needle and thread.

He laughed, running his hand through his hair, dislodging bits of plaster onto the bed. "You're probably wondering why my market day clothes got in this state." He rose and rummaged in the chest at the foot of his bed, getting fingerprints all over the newly polished wood, before producing a needle and thread. "I was so excited a few weeks ago by the prospect of my new method that I fell to work immediately and forgot to change."

I shook my head as I made quick work of the torn cuff.

"What's your name? You have a name?" He wiped a bit of dried clay from his forehead. "Mine is Bernard. In case you've forgotten."

I would have liked to say I couldn't possibly have forgotten. I would have liked to tell him a great many things. He should hire an apprentice or two, to help him with all the commissioned earthenware orders he was receiving. He should buy another shirt, trim his hair, build prettier shelves in his front windows, and serve tea for the fashionable ladies who were so fond of his pottery, but I could not.

"Do you write?"

I bowed my head. I wished I could.

"Read?"

I continued to stitch his torn cuff back together in neat, invisible stitches. *No.*

"But you have a name."

I paused long enough to glare at him. *Of course I have a name!*

"Well, then, if I am to guess, the least you could do is give me a clue."

I would not form the words, much as I wanted to, but I did gesture to the lantern on his bedside table.

"Lantern? Lantern is your name?"

I rolled my eyes and put down my mending.

"Light. Lumière."

I spun my forefingers around and around. *Keep going. Almost there.*

"Licht. Leggera."

No, but so close!

"Lux." He blew out a breath. "Liticia. Lucinda. Lucia."

I melted at the sound of my name on his lips, before smiling and frantically nodding.

"Which one? Liticia? Lucia?"

I reached for his hands and squeezed them. *Yes, Lucia.* Astrid Lucia, but I'd happily answer to just Lucia. It was as much my name as Astrid.

"Lucia." He cocked his head. "That's a pretty name."

And I had a pretty face and an even prettier curse to match. I resumed my mending, stabbing the needle with more force than needed.

"What happened to you, Lucia?" he asked quietly.

I looked up, pausing midstitch.

"Forgive me. My mouth says things before I can stop to think."

What a luxury.

"Have you always been like this?" he asked. "Not..." He blushed as his gaze darted to the clean windows. "I mean, I know grown women do not step out of seashells and travel for days to the mountains. Your voice, I mean. Has it always been a turncoat?"

I took a deep breath, but shook my head. *No. No, my voice has not always been a turncoat.*

His hands came over mine, stilling the work of my needle. "An accident?"

Something like that, my wan smile said.

"May I?" He brought his fingers up slowly to my jaw, sliding them over my neck, pausing at the scars he found there. "A burn, yes?"

I swallowed and nodded. Hot iron and flame were remedies I had tried.

His hands retreated.

I tied my thread and bit it off, handing him the shirt. He continued to stare at me. I shook it slightly at him.

He smiled. "Yes, I will remember to change next time." He sighed. "Deliveries tomorrow, I suppose, which means we shall see soon enough if I can afford both your wares and your washing."

CHAPTER THREE

I didn't return for two days, but when I did, Bernard greeted me with the embrace of a man whose fortunes had changed. At least he was wearing an apron now.

"All of them. All of them sold." He took my hands and moved them until they formed a cup. He then filled them with gold. "I want all the same creatures as before, but more. The ladies want complete matching sets. I'll set the beasties in different poses. Create vignettes and little family groups."

I smiled. Until I marked his windows. All were splattered with fresh mud.

"Oh," Bernard said, chuckling softly. "Oh dear." His eyes followed my gaze to the windows. "They are a mess. Well, it can't be helped. I have more commissions than I can count. I'll be so busy I'll barely have enough time to eat…" His smile turned sheepish. "You cook too, yes?"

I rolled my eyes, but got to work. Although his bedchamber was in a state again, it would take only an hour or so to remedy this time. His pantry was a different story—unsealed jars of salt and spices, stale flour, day-old bread, and half-eaten cheese. Where were the dried herbs, the curing vegetables? It was midsummer. Piles of squashes and onions should have been lining these shelves. As it was, the chickens were getting the best of his harvest.

The man was a hopeless housekeeper, but he knew his craft. And he was ambitious, creative, healthy, handsome—even with the messy beard and clay in his eyelashes. Kind and fair, and he hadn't soured on me yet, despite my snakes and lizards.

Who taught you? I asked by gesturing to his studio and the small portrait on the wall near his dining table.

Bernard had invited me to stay for supper, although only after he'd seen that I'd set the table for two.

"Oh, we've always been potters. I was born in the bed upstairs. Same as my father and his father before. I was at the wheel before I could walk."

I looked around. "*We*"?

"This house is too empty. I think it's what inspired me to use all your little friends in my work. Add more life..." He stabbed his fork into the pile of food on his plate. "My sister, Maria, married well five years ago. Sometimes I see her husband on market day. A baker now, but gracious, you'd think she and Timothy were making lace with how done up their pastries look."

I wanted to ask about his parents, but Bernard just chewed and stared into space.

"Do you have family?" he asked after another bite.

The food in my mouth turned to ash. I had, once. Before my curse ripped them away from me. I should have shaken my head and smiled. That would have been easier than the truth. But Bernard watched me too closely for lies.

"A sister?" he pressed. "I have a sister, so I know the look."

My shoulders slumped. I nodded. *Once upon a time, yes. I had a sister.*

"Older? Or younger?"

I winced, knocking over my cup of water. The memory of Violet's horror-stricken face was like a flash of lightning in my mind—abrupt, powerful, but mercifully fleeting.

Bernard rose and returned with a towel. "Not to worry." He blotted the table dry. "I've never been one to fuss over a little mess." He winked at me before refilling my cup and returning to his chair.

"I say." He took another enormous mouthful of food. "This is delicious. What did you do to this bird?"

I'd roasted his fattest chicken with leeks and onions and seasoned it with some of the salt that surely would not store past the summer. Dressed with sautéed squash and some of the fresh herbs that had been choked by the weeds in his gardens—it was the finest meal I'd prepared in ages.

"Laundress, cook, huntress of rare specimens..." He squinted out the window, and his eyes widened when he saw his neatly tended garden. "And grounds keeper. Is there anything you don't do?"

I smiled wryly and patted the front of my neck.

Bernard laughed. "Apart from the obvious."

After that, I took Bernard a small basket of creatures every morning throughout summer. It was easier to keep his house tidy and his kitchens well stocked if I was there every day. Never mind that I enjoyed the sight of the man. Or that I found his house comforting when he was lost in thought at his wheel and I was occupied with the washing or cooking.

"Did you plant geraniums in my window boxes?" he asked one afternoon as he splashed his hands in the basin of water next to his wheel and coaxed a teapot out of the spinning cone of clay.

I didn't nod. Instead, I glanced sidelong at the pink geraniums that now adorned the window boxes on the front of his home. After I'd tamed the garden, I'd turned my attention to the front of his house—weeding and smartening. I had hauled up new dirt from the creek bed and spent a silver coin on each of the hothouse flowers on market day. Their cheerful, bold color was plainly visible from the open windows of the studio. It was no surprise Bernard hadn't noticed the flowers before.

My smile, sly and small, was commentary on the length of time it'd taken Bernard to notice the flowers. A complete fortnight. His lack of attention to everything that was not his craft was infuriating, confounding.

And charming.

"They're pretty," he said, holding my gaze. "The sort of uncomplicated pretty that you come to depend on." He straightened and attended to the clay on his wheel, wetting his hands before grazing his fingers along the twirling shape. "The kind of pretty you hope stays forever."

Heat crept up from my heart into my neck.

"I want to go with you tonight. When you capture the creatures."

My lips twisted into a playful smile. I imitated his heavy footfalls and shook my head. I created the smallest hole I could with my fingers curled in a fist and peered through them at Bernard, demonstrating how my fingers could easily slide in. I took Bernard's hand away from the clay at his wheel and measured its size, showing how even his little finger was too big.

Bernard smiled down at our hands. "I'm too loud and too big and would scare all the little creatures away. Is that what you're saying?"

I nodded, my heart catching as he rubbed his clay-covered thumb against my palm.

"Very well, Lucia. Away with you to hunt the little beasts. But fair warning." His lips quirked into a smile before his attention turned again to the clay on the wheel. "I will ask again."

I returned the next morning, trying my best not to look wan and stricken. I was dizzy with exhaustion and overwhelmed by the aches of my tired muscles.

Bernard was too enthralled with my captured wares to notice. "This one is venomous. I'm sure of it! Look at the striking colors. And this one!" He lifted the glass lizard. "I've never seen a snake with ears and eyelids."

A fortnight later, as the sun set and I was preparing to leave for the night, he asked again to accompany me.

"Let me come." His fingers grazed my wrist. His touch was playful and bold. He stooped in the hall, a single shoulder leaning against the plaster wall.

I smiled, enjoying the warmth of his hands even if they were caked in mud.

"Who cares if you catch any beasts? I have work enough as it is." He took a step closer. His lips were so close to mine.

I didn't move. I didn't want to move.

"Lucia, it isn't fair for you to have all the fun and leave me here." He brushed a single clean knuckle down the length of my braid. "Alone."

I pressed my hand to his cheek, his beard bristling against my palm. I smiled as Bernard closed his eyes and leaned into my touch. I waited until I had his full attention, then shook my head. *No.*

"But I'll be up all night thinking of you anyway."

I grinned. Good, but my answer was still no.

CHAPTER FOUR

I continued to go to Bernard's daily even as the nights lengthened and the summer grass dried and bleached. He paid me each morning for my wares and paid me after every market day for the washing and cooking.

"I don't need more beasts," Bernard said the morning of an unseasonably early frost.

My pulse thrummed in my ears. Had he at last soured on my wares?

"I've taken more casts than I have customers."

I slammed my basket of toads and snakes on his worktable. *Fine.*

Bernard rocked on his bare feet before rubbing the back of his neck. "I know I pay you for the washing and cooking, but what I need is a proper housekeeper."

My jaw clenched, and the studio became uncomfortably quiet.

"I can't keep you on like this." He attempted a weak smile that looked almost shy. Had the man never dismissed anyone before? Didn't he know that smiles were unnecessary when he'd already made up his mind about what he wanted?

I grabbed my basket and stormed out to the vegetable garden.

He followed. "Lucia?"

I overturned my basket, watching the snakes writhe before darting for shelter under the wilted squash and melon vines. The toads, poor things, lay there on the frosted ground exactly as they fell, some on their sides, some upside down. Too stunned and too stupid to flee. I knew the feeling well.

I fell to my knees. I wanted to cry. I wanted to say all manner of words that couldn't be spoken. A *proper housekeeper*? As if the miracles I'd worked scrubbing mud from every surface of that house weren't proof enough of my skill and dedication.

I started ripping up the plants that had withered in the frost.

"Lucia!" Bernard knelt next to me. His hand reached for mine, but I pulled back. "I can't bear the thought of you hunting creatures alone now that the nights have turned cold."

And I couldn't bear the thought of leaving. I pulled up a melon vine, breaking it into manageable lengths and shaking the dirt from the roots over Bernard's head before dusting my palms and rising.

"Where are you going?" he asked.

I didn't know, and it didn't matter. I was leaving.

He beat me to the back door, slamming it shut in my face. "I have enough money saved to pay you handsomely all winter."

I swatted him out of the way, pushing against the door with my hip, but he held it closed. "More will come in. If it doesn't, I'll figure something out."

I frowned. What was he talking about?

He took me by the shoulders. "Stay on as my housekeeper. You can have your pick of any of the rooms upstairs, including mine." He swallowed, his hands sliding from my shoulders down my arms until my hands were cradled in his. "I can't lose you. Not to a frost. Not to another household that would offer you a proper position. Please, Lucia. Stay with me. I need you."

Oh, the stupid fool of a man. My shoulders relaxed. I closed my eyes and nodded. *Yes, of course.*

"That means you'll live here as a proper housekeeper. Sleep here?"

My mouth quirked into a smile. I gestured at the morning sun and held up a single finger.

"Fine, after tonight." A small snake wriggled under the collar of Bernard's shirt. I pulled the little fellow out and placed him gently on a sunny rock.

"It must have been part of that shower of dirt you shared with me earlier," he said, checking his beard, hair, and trousers for more.

My smile was broad.

"Sorry, I meant to say 'the well-deserved shower.'"

Later that night, deep in the woods, I repeated his words again and again, knowing they might be the last I ever spoke. "Please, Lucia. Stay with me. I need you."

I should have left that summer, but Bernard's earthenware was popular, and his touch was kind.

I should have left the first time he kissed me. A clumsy, bumbled brush of lips accompanied by mud stains on my waist where he pulled me close. I smiled when I scrubbed out those stains on wash day.

"Marry me, Lucia," Bernard said against my temple the second time I let him kiss me.

No, my eyes said. I brought his hands to my neck, to the red welts that never quite faded from when I'd tried to burn the curse away. I kissed his hand and traced his fingers over the scars from the stinging nettles I'd worn for weeks, hoping they, too, would be a cure.

I can't, my tears said.

"I don't care, if that's what you're worried about. Truly. I have better conversations with you than anyone. You listen. And you sass and chide and flirt." He pressed a kiss to my cheek. "Your silence never feels empty." He rested his forehead to mine. "I'm learning my letters, slowly. But after I learn, I can teach you. In time, we could write and read and…" He swallowed. "Will you think about it?"

I couldn't *not* think about it. A home, not just when geraniums bloomed in the window boxes, but for always. And the promise of words, not spoken but written. Was it even possible?

I stood in Bernard's door early the next morning as he tumbled out of bed and splashed water on his face.

I held my cloak in my hand and showed him my basket packed with fresh fruit, cheese, honeycomb, and bread.

"How long will you be gone?" Bernard asked, pulling me into his arms. He smelled of clay, but also the sweetness of an afternoon in the autumn sun. Once the snow started and sunshine retreated, washing the linens would be a challenge.

I held up three fingers.

"Three nights?"

I kissed his cheek, which earned me a small smile.

"I'll ask again when you return."

If I returned, I'd say yes and marry him. If I returned.

"Hurry back."

I walked until I reached the neighboring village. There, I hired a cart and a mule—easy to do with a purse full of coin. All day, I traveled east through farmlands, meadows, and forests. The road, though never steep, sloped upward the entire journey. When at last I stopped at the foot of a mountain stream, the sky had faded to a dull purple, the last tired light of evensong bathing all in the gray of old wash water. I rubbed the mule's neck and let the beast drink before tying him to a tree. I'd have to continue up the mountain on foot.

Unlike fairies, witches were easy to find. Everyone knew where to find a witch. They made no point of hiding.

The half-moon was high overhead when at last I came to a small cottage that had a smoking chimney. I knocked sharply on the door, and when there was no answer, I knocked again.

"Go away!" a voice shrieked from within.

"No!" My stomach knotted and tightened. Sweat beaded on my forehead. I knocked incessantly until I heard shuffling.

The door creaked open, and an old woman, with hair like wires and eyebrows like feathers, greeted me. "Well?" the witch demanded.

I thrust my untouched basket of food under her nose, dropping in several gold coins that clattered against the jar of honeycomb, before I barged inside. I needed a bucket, a bowl, a vase, anything and fast. I spied a pot by the fire, dumped out the potatoes it contained, and held the cold iron against my middle.

"Good mother," I said, my voice catching against my shallow breaths. "I seek—"

My stomach writhed. I tried to swallow and breathe. I tried not to think of what would come. The first bout of the night was always the cruelest. "I seek your counsel."

A shiver slid up my spine, and my stomach twisted. I retched a half-dozen acorn-size toads into the pot. I shuddered. "Does this pot have a..." I heaved and heaved again before expelling a warty toad. "A lid?" I gasped, panting.

The woman shuffled to a cupboard opposite the hearth and rummaged a moment before shoving a tarnished copper lid under my nose. "You'll be scrubbing them both clean before you go." She settled in her rocking chair. "A mercy I read the tea leaves and put the cats out before you came. Better tell me what all this is about before they return." The old woman ceased her rocking. "You don't cough up mice, do you?"

I parted my lips, but thought it better to simply shake my head.

"Well, that's a mercy too." The witch sighed and wrinkled her nose, then picked up her knitting needles. "A curse, is it?"

"Have you ever known a woman to vomit toads naturally?" My voice was hoarse.

The witch chuckled.

My stomach cramped, and a tremor shook my frame. "I crossed a fairy."

"You don't say?" the witch said, looping wool around her clicking needles. "Bet it was a pretty one. All the worst curses come from pretty fairies."

"Her many silk skirts were the only pretty thing about her." I felt the slither up my throat and lifted the lid of the pot just in time to spit out a snake.

The witch's hands paused, her sharp eyes fixing on my own. "Snakes too?"

I grimaced and clutched my stomach. "All manner of reptiles and amphibians."

She resumed her knitting, her needles rhythmically clacking against each other. "So your saucy tongue got you in trouble with a fairy. Why?"

I closed my eyes, trying to calm the churning of my stomach. "She cursed my little sister."

"Gracious, there's another one of you out there spitting snakes?"

Sweat trickled down my back. "She retches diamonds." I winced, and my stomach twisted with acute nausea before the heaving started again. "Gems and flowers, too." A cascade of snakes tumbled into the pot.

I spat out a small frog, closing the lid as I wiped my mouth. "But she's just as sick and miserable as I am when it happens." I shivered, but not because of another spasm. The memory of Violet, pale and shaking on her little bed as Mama demanded more words filled me with rage. "Worse, if you can believe it." I coughed and hacked up another couple of toads. I pressed my hands to my middle and whimpered. So many toads tonight. "Violet's always been small." *Delicate* was the word Mama used. *Delicate is fashionable*, Mama's voice echoed in my mind, *in ways sickly and small can never be.*

I groaned and closed my eyes. "'A blessing,' Mama said. That's why she sent me to the well. She was hoping I'd get a blessing of my own. It wasn't enough that one daughter was filling buckets with riches every day. She needed two." I retched more snakes into the pot and shuddered. "Do you have another? This one's nearly full." I coughed. "I'd hate for it to spill over. You keep a tidy cottage."

Polished floor, clean-swept hearth, drying herbs hanging in pretty bundles from the timbers overhead. Shelves with neat rows of glass bottles that winked in the firelight. This was the type of place I only ever dared dream about when I was lying cold and alone in my hovel. A place that was dry, warm, and clean. A place where there could be order and, in time, beauty because of permanence.

My dreams hadn't changed since meeting Bernard.

The witch moved quickly, overturning her knitting basket and handing me a folded quilt to use as a lid.

"Thank you," I said, trying to breathe through the cramps in my stomach. "The frogs like to jump."

The witch grimaced. "So you met this fairy and politely asked that your sister's gift be removed?"

I leveled a pained stare at the witch before lying down in front of her hearth. "I poured the bucket of well water on her when she asked me for a drink. Then I demanded she remove Violet's curse."

The witch chuckled.

I groaned, scrunching up my nose and pitching my voice all shrill like the fairy's had been. "'I'll show you a curse!'"

I scrambled upright before ejecting a glass snake into the knitting basket. It was large and long. My eyes streamed with tears when at last I covered the basket with the blanket. "I shouldn't have laughed when she said that. But she was dripping wet and looked for all the world like a drowned rabbit." I dry heaved after that, until at last a small ribbon snake wriggled out of my mouth. "They get smaller as the night goes on," I said between gasps.

"Enough, dear," the witch said, helping me to my feet. "You rest now and let old Gertrude fill in the details."

She led me to her little bed against the wall. It was luxurious, with a down mattress and finely woven linen sheets. I collapsed on it.

"I take it the retching stops if you do not speak?"

I nodded, trying to take slower, deeper breaths.

The witch rocked in her chair, her needles moving quietly. "And I take it your mama doesn't appreciate your gift from this fairy?"

I sighed. That was the worst of it, the terror and disgust on the faces of the people I loved. I could have shouldered Mama's disgust—her contempt for me was nothing new. But even the memory of Violet's horror was too much to bear.

"Wicked, vile girl," Mama shrieked from atop the table. Mama had never been a fan of snakes. "You are a monster. I knew it too. I knew you were always bad on the inside. Leave and never come back!"

"I'm not leaving Violet!" I yelled, before doubling over and vomiting toads. But Violet didn't want me either.

She hid in a corner of the bed we shared, sobbing.

"Violet?" She was so small, barely eight years old. I pulled the sheet away from my shaking sister. Her eyes were shut tight.

"Go away!" she screamed and retched diamonds all over the sheets.

"But, Violet, it's me, Astrid. Your sister." Maybe if I hadn't regurgitated lizards and snakes on top of her diamonds, she wouldn't have said the things she did.

"You aren't my sister!" She spewed out wet snowdrops. "You're a monster!" She was sobbing and hysterical and screaming so fiercely I was afraid she might shatter like glass. "I never want to see you again!"

My skin crawled at the memory. I breathed shallowly, trying to calm my stomach and keep the nausea from returning.

Gertrude sat deep in thought. She glanced at the covered basket on the floor and the pot, its lid periodically tittering. She pulled a deep bowl from her cupboard and placed it beside me along with a plate from her table. "To use as a lid," she explained. "Do you know the fairy's name?"

I shook my head.

"As I thought. I suppose you didn't make many friends before you learned the limits of your curse. Run out of a few towns, I'd take it."

I closed my eyes, trying not to remember. Dust comes out of an old cloak easily with washing. Spit—and other waste—takes more scrubbing.

"I'm guessing you learned quickly how to get by without speaking. I'm sure it wasn't easy, but you managed." Gertrude set her needles aside. "You've too much fire inside of you to be snuffed out by any curse."

I scoffed at that. I was a dying ember that had survived this long only because I'd found a potter who needed me as much as I needed him.

The witch poured a glass of water from the pitcher at her table and brought it to me. "And now... Something has changed, yes?"

I gratefully accepted the glass.

The witch almost smiled, but the corners of her lips pulled into a concerned frown. "The little ones..." She gestured to the pot and basket. "Will they need water?"

I shook my head.

The witch's eyes grew wide. "Will they eat each other?"

I shrugged, but rose to my feet. The glass snake was nosing its way out from under the blanket. I scooped it up, the beast twisting around my wrist, before it could slither under the witch's stove. With my free hand, I lifted the ribbon snake coiled in the bottom of the basket, opened the witch's front door, and set them both free.

"Leave the pot, dear," Gertrude said as she added red wool to her needles. "I'll sift through it in the morning. I've been meaning to boil some more toads before the ponds freeze." She returned to her rocking chair, and I returned to my seat in front of her hearth. "Now tell me what's changed. Have you met someone?"

I smiled, my skin warming at my waist where Bernard had held me yesterday.

"A young man, is it? I thought so. And you want to know if you can kiss him without snakes slithering into his mouth."

No. I winced. *Of course not.*

"Then you want to know how to break this spell." The witch counted the stitches on her needle. "I see boiling water, hot irons, and stinging nettles were of no help."

I took a deep breath. I had no other way to communicate what had to be said. "I don't care about breaking the curse." I heaved speckled salamanders into the empty basket at my side. Good. At least I didn't have to worry about them jumping out. "I need to know if I'll be able to write without starting all this business," I said, then spat out at least a dozen worm-sized striped corn snakes.

The witch blinked at me. "You don't care—"

"Breaking curses is a fool's errand. I've no time to waste on riddles or quests." This time, spotted frogs tumbled into the basket. "Bernard wants to marry me. He doesn't care that I can't speak."

"You mean 'won't speak.'" The witch looped the red wool around her needles in a complicated pattern. "You can speak. You choose not to in front of others."

I spat out a green lizard. Lizards were terrible. Their little legs and long tails often got stuck in my throat. They were not the worst, though. Turtles were the worst. I'd nearly choked to death on the shell of the last one I'd brought up. Thank the merciful heavens they were rare.

I shuddered and wiped the spit from my chin. I was disgusting, a woman who turned into a revolting monster whenever she spoke. "No man alive would want to bed a woman with snakes and toads crawling out of her mouth."

"What is your name, child?"

"Astrid," I said after coughing up a lizard with a tail twice as long as its body. "Astrid Lucia, after both my grandmothers." I gagged and expelled a pair of blind newts. "Although Mama said I was never good enough to deserve two names and only ever called me Astrid."

"Astrid Lucia, you give men more credit than they deserve."

I nearly laughed, but my breath was far from steady and my stomach still too sick to risk it. "Bernard wants to marry. He's learning to read and write so he can teach me. I need to know that I won't start retching when I put words to paper."

The witch frowned. "Wouldn't it be better to free yourself of this curse altogether?"

"Why? I have a chance at happiness now. A comfortable life with a good man."

"Do you love him?"

"What?" I whimpered, my stomach tightening.

"True love often works wonders for curses." Gertrude spread her knitting across her knees, fingering the intricate stitches and the fresh rows of red wool against the cream. "Love makes us brave, encourages us to take risks. A life without risks, Astrid Lucia, is not a life worth living."

"Are you saying I should tell Bernard about my curse?" I would have laughed in the witch's face if I'd had the strength. "I'm not going to risk losing him, my home and livelihood all at once."

Gertrude wove a loose end of wool into her knitting. "I'm only asking. Do you love him?"

I stared down at the basket I held of writhing snakes, salamanders, lizards, newts, and toads. I was fond of Bernard. He was clever and generous. He was endearingly hopeless when it came to everything that made life comfortable and tidy, and... He needed me. I savored that need. After years of being unwanted and despised, that need was everything. Now need had grown into something even more intoxicating—want. Bernard wanted me, and I needed him. It was enough, and I didn't dare ask for more.

"I'm sure I could love him in time. Particularly if he ever learns to wash the clay out of his hair before he falls into bed." It was a bluff. I wasn't sure of anything. It didn't matter. I'd already spoken too many words that night. I paid for them dearly, filling both the basket and the basin on the bed with more creatures.

The witch considered. She brought her hands together, folding them under her chin, then unfolding them and spreading them out across the arms of her rocking chair. "You've built a life you are satisfied with."

I nodded.

"You don't wish for this life to change? You only want to know if written words are included in your curse?"

Exactly.

The witch sighed. "You learned the haggler signs for market day?"

Of course.

"Show me three crowns, four silver pennies," she said.

I held up three fingers before touching my thumb to my littlest finger. I held up four fingers before touching my thumb to my middle finger.

"And you've always been able to communicate consent by nodding and shaking your head without coughing up so much as a single toad?"

Always.

The witch frowned. "You are lucky. You are very lucky this fairy was preoccupied with your saucy tongue and not your saucy mind. I've seen curses that are triggered whenever someone opens their mouth or even thinks."

A scratching and meowing came from the window behind the rocking chair. The witch unlatched it, and a couple of bright-eyed black cats strutted in, tails and whiskers twitching.

"You can write your potter sonnets or dirty limericks, fill pages and pages with all the words you know. Nothing will change. Your curse will not be triggered."

Relief spread over me. "Thank you, good mother." I belched, and a fat skink with a bright blue tail tumbled into the basket.

"Help me sort the venomous from the tame?" the witch said, tossing a couple of harmless frogs from the iron pot for the cats. "Now, mind you don't leave any crumbs," she said to the felines, "or I'll throw you both out until the new moon."

I quickly pulled the brightest of the creatures from the basket and pots and put them in the crocks the witch had pulled from her oven.

The sun was just cresting the mountain when we finished.

We ambled down the mountainside to my borrowed mule. "Thank you, Gertrude." I bent over and coughed up what I hoped was the last toad of my life.

"Good luck, Astrid Lucia."

I thanked her with more coins from my purse.

Gertrude frowned as she jangled the coins in her wrinkled hand. "Worse than the tea leaves," she muttered.

My eyebrows drew up. I knew that reading tea leaves was a means of fortune-telling, but could the same be done with gold and silver coins?

She jangled the coins again, her lips twitching as she traced the different patterns the coins made. "I fear you won't be able to keep your curse secret from the potter forever. Marriage is not a union of bits and pieces, but of whole selves."

My brow furrowed. What was the old witch talking about? Maybe a younger, sillier woman would be tempted or tricked by romantic ideals, but years of cold, hungry nights had stamped such nonsense out of me. Marriage was what any two people needed it to be, and that was enough for me.

Gertrude sighed before tucking the coins into her pocket, rattling them in place. "Suit yourself, but heed my parting words of warning. Don't return to the market with your husband, Astrid Lucia. Things will never be the same if you do."

CHAPTER FIVE

I traveled all that day. The sun was hot. The roads were dusty. The mule was tired. We went slow, stopping at every shady brook I could find. I didn't mind that we didn't make good time. I was turning over the witch's words in my head.

I might not be able to speak for the rest of my life, but in time, I'd be able to read and write with impunity. I'd have a home and a husband who wanted as well as needed me. It would be enough. I didn't want more.

Gertrude was wrong. I had learned to live with my curse. I could spend the rest of my life in silence. I could be married and keep my curse a secret forever.

At dusk, I returned the borrowed mule and cart and bought a room at the village inn for the night. A warm meal, a cool bath, a soft bed—it all should have been enough to ensure a night of rest, but I could not sleep. Hours before daybreak, I plaited my hair and donned my cloak.

It was still dark when I arrived at the potter's house. I let myself in quietly and was surprised to find Bernard at his wheel, a single lit lantern swinging idly above him, casting lazy shadows across his studio.

I stood at the edge of that light, admiring the corded muscles of his forearms, the dexterity of his fingers as he drew one shape after another out of the clay. His actions looked like legerdemain, something a conjurer would do at a festival to draw a crowd and earn some coin. Children called such tricks magic, but magic was no sleight of hand. Magic was persistence mixed with skill and passion and something too slippery to chase.

Bernard looked up from his wheel for a moment. A smile danced across his lips. He'd been to the barber in my absence. His beard was trimmed closer to his jaw and away from his lips. He shook his head and returned his gaze to his wheel like I was an apparition, a whisper in his eye that had haunted him all summer or an echo that would remain at the corner of his lips for the rest of his life.

When I stepped closer, Bernard looked up again and blinked, lines forming between his brows.

Yes, my coy smile said. *Yes, I'm here.*

Bernard leaped to his feet in such haste his stool overturned. He bumped his worktable. A stack of dried bowls tumbled to the floor and shattered.

"Lucia." His hands were on my back, drawing me closer, pulling me in, until I could feel his heart beat against my breast. "I didn't think I'd ever see you again."

He held me for a moment, resting his forehead against mine. I savored the smell of him, earthy and sweet. My lips skated across his cheek as I turned to rest my head against his shoulder.

His hands moved to the sides of my face, whispering across my cheeks. I closed my eyes, and his lips brushed, soft and slow, against each of my eyelids. "And here you are." He kissed me then, his lips shaking against mine. "My Lucia."

I tipped my chin up, and Bernard pressed another unhurried kiss to my neck. I arched my back and threaded my fingers into the locks of hair at the nape of his neck.

His kisses trailed down to my collarbone. "You came back early. If I'd known, I would have washed up, picked flowers, sent for one of Timothy and

Maria's pretty cakes." He paused and looked at me. A moment of hesitation. A moment to let me ease out of his embrace...if I wanted.

I didn't.

"Marry me, Lucia. I don't want to spend another day or night without you."

A cricket chirped outside the closed window. The lantern had ceased swaying now that the wheel was still. I didn't think about the morning, when I'd scrub the glass panes and clean up the dripping wax and shattered pottery. The pleasure of being wanted was too distracting. My lips quirked into a smile. *Yes,* I nodded. I rose on tiptoe to kiss Bernard's lips. Yes, I'd marry him. Why else did he think I had come back?

Bernard let out a bemused, winded laugh before he took me in his arms and kissed me again. If his kisses had been like a gentle rain shower before, they were a downpour of heavy, roaring rain now, a surprise thunderstorm that fell so fast and hard I would remember it for the rest of my life. Rain that took my breath away and made the blood rush inside of me until I was sure the deafening pounding I heard was my own pulse. Rain so thrilling, so exciting and terrifying, I hoped it would never stop.

We stumbled, a tangle of connected lips and intertwined limbs, bumping against the tables and tools in his studio, drowning in each other's kisses. "I missed you," Bernard panted. His breath was hot against my neck.

I returned his kisses, near drunk on the feeling of being wanted. Of knowing that every part of him hungered for me.

"I counted the hours," Bernard said. "I would have wept for joy yesterday if I'd known you were returning a whole day early."

I couldn't wait, my kisses said.

Bernard pressed me closer, kissed me, stumbled with me in his arms until my back was against the wall of his studio. The lantern was swaying again above us, catching us now and then in brighter light. It was then I noticed the mud stains on Bernard's shoulders, in his hair, on his chest, in his beard, at his waist. Because I'd braced myself more than once against his clay-covered worktables as we kissed, my hands were caked in mud and leaving trails all over Bernard. I glanced down and realized my clothing had fared no better. We were both covered in mud, and for once, I didn't care. I kissed him again.

"You sure about this?" His fingers toyed with the strings of my cloak.

I smiled against his lips. *Yes.* I pulled him closer, kissing him deeply, feeling my stomach tighten and turn in the same way it had when I'd first seen him that day in the market.

He hesitated for the briefest of moments before picking me up.

I kissed his neck, but inhaled sharply when he carried me outside instead of up the stairs. I squirmed. Where were we going?

"The priest will already be awake. Better make it official before the sun is up and you see what a mess we've made."

I should have been mortified. Dressed as I was, splattered in mud, and about to be married. Instead, I shook with silent laughter.

"My children," the priest said when Bernard carried me into the church. "Has there been an accident? Some sort of mudslide? Did the maiden break an ankle?"

Bernard set me down, pinching my waist when I could not hide my smirk. "We wish to marry."

The priest looked dismayed, confused.

Bernard tossed him a pouch of coins. "Now, if you please."

I'd worried that Bernard would grow bored of me in the months that followed our marriage. That he'd tire of my attention. That he would become accustomed to my affection the same as he'd grown accustomed to my housekeeping.

He didn't. My steady presence didn't change his need or his want. It remained with the same certainty as a coastal tide, rising and falling, but ever present at the seashore. I continued to enjoy cosseting Bernard. Our life, our home, was too precious for carelessness. Mending, polishing, washing, cooking, scrubbing, gardening, tending, patching. I'd learned all manner of skills living for years alone in the woods, and I put them all to good use in our home.

Bernard continued to create earthenware with the casts he'd made of the creatures. He ventured, too, into finer work that referenced only the intricate pattern of the beasts' colored scales. These were smooth, delicate pieces that required a steady hand that came only from being well fed, well rested, and well bedded. Each dish was thinner than snake bone, and each sold for a small fortune.

We bought a new cart with glass cabinets for market day. I helped Bernard pack his wares every week, but I never accompanied him.

"Please, Lucia." Bernard begged me every time. "Come with me. You don't know how I miss you."

I knew. There was no mistaking how much he missed me when he greeted me at day's end. Truthfully, I missed him, too, but not as much as I savored that his want for me grew in our hours apart. Besides, I wasn't about to ignore Gertrude's warning. I didn't want anything to change. We were too happy—I was too happy—to take any risks by attending market days.

That fall, we enjoyed all of the manifestations of love and emblems of devoted hearts. And yet, despite my fondness, despite our mutual attachment and need, something was missing. Was it love? My curse prevented me from declaring any such feeling, but even if I could speak, would I say the words? Bernard had not, and I feared it was because I had not truly claimed his heart nor he mine. It didn't matter, I reasoned. What we had was enough.

"Come with me to the solstice festival," Bernard said. "How will I survive the darkest, coldest, longest night of the year without my wife?"

I dusted the kitchen table with flour, but paused long enough to give Bernard a look—*the* look. The one that said if he valued marital bliss, he'd better not push.

"I've never sold my pottery at the capital, and Maria says it is not a one-man job."

I tipped the bowl of bread dough onto the table. Wasn't that why Bernard was partnering with Timothy and Maria and sharing their festival stall? Fancy plates for fancy pastries? Fancy pastries for fancy plates?

"Timothy and Maria have invited us to stay with them," Bernard said, wrapping his arms around me and resting his chin on my shoulder.

I continued to knead the bread dough. My days were too busy now that there were only so many hours of sunshine. Besides, I wasn't about to freeze on the road to the capital just to stand outside in a festival stall, freezing some more. Never mind old Gertrude's warning about markets, I was poor company and an even poorer saleswoman, especially when the weather turned cold and wet. Bernard was the only loyal customer I'd ever had.

"I will miss you all week, and I will have no one to talk to if the weather turns poor and business is slow."

I smiled at Bernard before throwing the dough on the table. I knew he would miss me. I still was not going.

"The winter solstice festival is so big and so loud no one can understand anyone even if they do speak. Pointing, gesturing. Three fingers up for the price. A thumbs-up for the sale. It's all any of us will be able to do." Bernard spun me around and kissed the corner of my lips. "I'll sell twice as much with you there. Your pretty eyes will catch all the fine gentlemen's attention."

I swatted Bernard's shoulder. I had work to do.

"Please." Bernard pulled a chair out from the table and sat. "I know you hate markets, and I don't blame you." He gently caught my flour-dusted wrist and pulled me onto his lap, pressing sweet kisses to my temple. "They're a tedious business. But this is the solstice festival. This is different. People travel for miles to attend. There are all manner of wonders in addition to the vendors like me. Contortionists who can fold themselves into boxes so small we could stack a half dozen on this table. Musicians who play with such skill and move their fingers so fast that steam rises from their instruments' strings. Illusionists who make grown men disappear. Snake charmers and lion tamers. Last year, Maria said there was even a camelopard with a neck so long it could ring the bell in the church steeple while standing in the town square."

My eyes narrowed. Gertrude had said nothing about festivals. *Don't return to the market with your husband, Astrid Lucia. Things will never be the same if you do.* That was what the witch had said. But a festival wasn't a market, and I would not be *returning* if I'd never been there before.

Bernard knew me too well not to notice my resolve weakening. His hand rubbed gentle circles at the base of my neck. "We'll be back before our village yule market even begins."

His hands moved to my own, where he caressed the same pattern of circles on my palm. My eyes drifted shut for a moment, savoring his gentleness.

"I swear, I will never ask you to come with me to the market again if you let me take you to the solstice festival." He pressed a kiss to the hinge of my jaw.

I sighed.

"Please, Lucia. Come with me. Don't you want to see a camelopard?" He kissed my palm.

Of course I wanted to see such a creature.

I placed a chaste kiss on Bernard's cheek, knowing full well I'd never get my bread rising in time for dinner if I kissed him any other way.

"You'll come?"

I winked at him, conceding my amused defeat.

"Oh! Lucia. You won't be sorry. We'll sell so much pottery we'll need to rent a horse and carriage to haul all the gold back with us."

I rolled my eyes and led him back to his wheel. If we were indeed to sell such quantities of pottery, he'd better keep working.

"And the food. Wait until you try Timothy's strudel."

I smoothed the hair away from his face, delighted by his enthusiasm.

"Who knows what other wonders we'll find?"

CHAPTER SIX

The solstice festival was exactly as Bernard had described. Well, the length of the camelopard's neck was far less impressive than Maria had indicated, but only because the bell tower of the capital's cathedral was three times as high as any bell tower either of us had ever seen. The beast absolutely would have been tall enough to eat the fir branches I'd tucked into the window boxes upstairs after the frost had killed the geraniums.

Fortune-tellers, minstrels, flame eaters, and all manner of entertainers lined the streets and commons of the capital. Glassblowers, soapers, cheesemongers, lacemakers, silversmiths, farmers, potters, and bakers were there in droves.

"It's a good thing you are the only potter who thought to make such unique pieces," Maria shouted at midday. "We're getting twice the foot traffic than the other bakers. Everyone wants to see your unusual wares."

I'd never heard such noise, seen so many people, or been so exhausted. That first night, I collapsed in Maria and Timothy's attic, falling dead asleep before even unlacing my boots.

"Lucia." Bernard woke me the next morning, holding a plate of pastry. A parcel was tucked under his arm. "Timothy's finest apple strudel." He kissed my temple as he handed me the plate. "I got you something. I saw it yesterday as we were setting up." He shook out the bundle and unfurled a beautiful fur-lined white cloak. "I wanted to buy it for you yesterday, but we got so busy and stayed open so late they'd already closed. Happy Yuletide." He knelt and wrapped the cloak, fine enough for a princess, around my shoulders. "I love you, Lucia."

My heart shattered with the words. I couldn't mask my shock, but I didn't have to, as Bernard was already climbing down the attic ladder.

Bernard loved me. He loved me, and my heart was now a raw, throbbing bundle, all soft and warm.

"Hurry, love. Timothy and Maria have already left."

"Love," I whispered. He called me love. I giggled softly but stopped immediately when I felt my stomach cramp. Oh no. I clamped a hand to my mouth, but it was too late. I was already gagging.

"Everything okay?" Bernard called.

I reached for the washbasin and promptly lost my breakfast, not stopping to mark what manner of creature came up with it. Not that it mattered—I heard the toad's croak as I unlatched the attic window and dumped the sick outside.

Bernard had a glass of water in his hand when I came down the attic ladder. "The strudel didn't agree with you?"

I nodded, wincing past the too sweet taste of the water.

"Not nearly as good as your fresh bread and apple butter, but don't tell Timothy I said that." Bernard took my hand, but stopped just shy of the door. "I almost forgot." He pulled out a pair of ceramic rings, each glazed in the same intricate pattern of diamonds and stripes as his finest pieces. "It took me longer than it should have to get these right." He slipped the smaller of the pair on my finger. "We can buy something prettier tomorrow if our sales are anything like they were yesterday. It's just ... I want everyone to know we're a matched set, you and I."

Bernard loved me, and I couldn't pretend any longer that I didn't love him. I took the larger ring and slid it on his finger, past his knuckle, giving it a quick kiss before I gave Bernard a longer one.

Maybe something like this was what the witch had seen in my fortune when she'd told me that things would change if I returned to the market with Bernard. Maybe it wasn't foreboding she'd seen, but glad tidings. Maybe I'd been afraid of a fate that was in fact too precious for words.

The winter sun was weak but dazzling as we walked to our stall. The streets were still uncrowded enough for us to walk hand in hand. I caught myself catching the sunshine winking off my new ring on more than one occasion. Bernard loved me, and this winter, the first thing I would learn to write would be the words *I love you too.*

"Astrid?"

I froze. My stomach dropped at the sound of that name.

"Astrid, is that you?" Violet, my sister, stood in the street, looking small and stricken. She wore a thin black dress that only barely covered her knees. It was an old dress that I had mended a dozen times. She should have outgrown it years ago in girth as well as height, but it hung loose from her shoulders, still too big in the middle.

I shielded my eyes from the sunshine, hoping Violet's pallor might be face paint or a trick of the light. The more garish flame breathers had mottled their faces with all manner of paints and creams yesterday. But this was no trick.

"Violet!" a shrill voice called. The streets were filling with more people, but I'd recognize that voice anywhere.

"Astrid." Violent grabbed my arm. Her grip was arrestingly tight, like the talons of a little lizard. "You have to help me. Please!" she shrieked.

"What's the matter?" Bernard's tone was amused, but he placed a protective arm around my shoulders. "Some act?"

"Please, help me. I'm begging—" Violet crumpled to the ground, spasming and shaking.

I grimaced as my little sister coughed up a puddle of slick flowers and gemstones.

Bernard's smile twisted into a frown. "What sort of act is this?"

I crouched, tentatively pressing my hand to Violet's neck, rubbing circles where I always ached the most when I was retching.

"Violet!" Mama, dressed in the most opulent of costumes and jewels, appeared in the crowd.

I straightened at the sight of that woman, and while I'd like to believe it was rage that made me shake, fear was far more likely.

Mama thrust a silk pouch in Violet's face. "You know performances are reserved for only the most exclusive of paying customers."

"Mama, it's Astrid!" Violet cried as she began scooping the wet gemstones into the pouch.

I wouldn't have recognized Mama in passing if she hadn't spoken. Her gaudy finery was blinding, but my mother was in fact underneath the rouge and yards of embroidered silk. Her eyes went wide when she saw me, and her lip curled. "Who, dear?"

"Astrid! Astrid!" Violet repeated. Her sobs were punctuated by wet coughs and the familiar rasps of someone fighting not to retch again. But it was no use. When she vomited next, forget-me-nots and emeralds fell from her lips to the cobbled street.

"Who is Astrid?" Bernard demanded.

"My sister!" Violet wailed before doubling over and expelling a bouquet's worth of goldenrod and delphinium.

Mama's eyes darted to the simple ceramic ring on my finger and then to Bernard's ring. Her expression was hard when she looked at me, undisguised anger and contempt on her face. I should have run when the sneer on her lips turned into a wide grin.

"Pardon my child, good sir. She was blessed by the fey some years ago. Flowers and diamonds fall from her pretty lips whenever she speaks."

"Astrid, please!" Violet begged. Tears streaked her ashen cheeks.

Mama cleared her throat forcefully. "Something of the magic has taken root in her mind, because she imagines her late sister, Astrid, everywhere."

The tension in Bernard's shoulders melted. "Grief and magic can weaken the mind."

"Exactly so," Mama said, nearly dragging Violet to her feet and herding her toward a tent behind a festival stall covered in flowers.

"No!" Violet shrieked, but she had none of Mama's strength or size. "Astrid, tell them!"

Mama pushed her forward, but Violet didn't make it to the tent. She fell to her knees, splattering diamonds across the wood floor of their market stall.

"Tell them who you are," Violet implored.

My eyes welled with tears, but tears were poor communicators, their meaning easily confused by other parties.

"My dear," Bernard said gently to Violet. "This is my wife, Lucia, and I'm afraid she's mute."

Mama cackled. She didn't even try to hide her derision.

Bernard pulled me closer, perhaps hoping to shield me from her cruelty. "Madam, it is nothing to laugh about."

"Astrid, save me! I don't want to travel with the festivals anymore. I want to rest. I want to—" Violet vomited again. This time garnets and sapphires.

"Monster," Violet wailed through tears.

I squeezed my eyes shut, the hurt of that word too raw even after three years.

Violet took quick, panicked breaths. "She's a monster. I've been sick every day since you left. I hate flowers. I hate diamonds." She spat out more stones. "I want to keep a meal down and not see it come up with rocks." Violet shook on her hands and knees. "You know what it is like living with a curse. Imagine if you couldn't find a moment's peace. Imagine being paraded like an animal in front of anyone who will pay, milked morning, noon, and night for the horrors you cough up."

"Madam, what is she talking about?" Bernard demanded.

"Inside," Mama said, pulling Violet to her feet and pushing her through the tent. She looked Bernard up and down, then did the same to me, before holding the tent flap open for us. "We will discuss this inside."

It was a trap. No good could come of walking into that tent. But Bernard was already marching forward, and my hand was still tucked tightly inside his.

It took my eyes a moment to adjust to the clash of oranges, purples, and reds of the tent's sumptuous interior. The light was dim, and so it took me longer to realize that everything was covered in gemstones. The surface of the tea table was adorned with deepest amethysts, blood-red agates, and other gems I could not name. The arms of the settee were decorated with a motley assortment of glittering fuchsia stones. Even its cushions were embroidered with more stones than I'd wager decorated the emperor's crown.

So many gems, and they'd all come from Violet. Small wonder she looked so sick.

"This is where we entertain our best customers." Mama struck a long match and lit the candles of the diamond-and-ruby chandelier that swayed above us.

Bernard gasped as the room sparkled to life. The tent held more riches than just the gems. Thick, silk Easterlie carpets covered the floor. Tapestries hung from the orange-, purple-, and red-striped walls. I frowned in disgust at one that portrayed a fair princess staring into a hand mirror, her eyes overlaid with diamonds in the reflection.

Mama blew out the match. "And where I discuss old family business, it would seem." She dragged a chair bejeweled with blue stones away from the tea table and reached for a crystal decanter filled with amber spirits on a nearby cart. She sat with an arm draped across the back of her chair as she poured a solitary glass from the decanter and downed it in a single gulp. "My eldest daughter was a proud, foolish girl. She insulted the same fairy Violet found favor with and was cursed." Mama sneered at me. "Fetch your sister a pail, will you?" She gestured to the far corner of the tent. "Can't have her sick all over the carpet. Rose petals leave especially nasty stains."

I did as I was told. As I bent to collect the rusted pail, I noticed that the tapestry that hung in this corner of the tent was a curtain. Behind it was a small dirty bed that rested on a bare dirt floor. My heart stopped when I saw the ball and chain beside the bed.

I set the bucket next to Violet, who lay, moaning and shivering, on the floor.

"Cursed, you say... Cursed like your daughter?" Bernard gestured with his chin at Violet.

My heart beat too loud in my ears while my breath grew shallow. People liked pretty things, and people liked the comfort that came with wealth. They didn't care if others suffered so long as they had their pretty riches. Let a poor girl writhe, so long as they didn't have to see it.

Cursed like your daughter? Was it an innocent question or one inlaid with all manner of greed and ambition? I didn't want to know. I unfastened my cloak and tucked it around Violet, taking special care of her bruised and cut ankles.

Mama cackled, heartless woman that she was. "Yes," she said.

Bernard's eyes grew as round as the plates he threw at his potter's wheel. My warm, tender heart felt like it was being squeezed until it was cold and lifeless.

"And no." Mama's mouth twisted into a grin so wide it drained the color from her lips.

All I could do was hold my breath, but if I could have, I would have stuffed Mama's throat with a viper.

Bernard frowned before he burst into hearty laughter. "Woman, you are clearly mad."

I breathed again. Bernard loved me. He cared for me. I was right to keep the madness of this curse away from our love. It had no place in our happy life.

"It's true!" Violet wailed. "I swear it's true." She rose to her elbows, vomiting peonies and lapis lazuli that clattered and plinked as they tumbled into the bucket. "Astrid. Sister! Tell him!"

I couldn't. If I spoke now, Bernard would see that I was a monster, and I'd lose the man I loved and everything besides. Someday, even if I managed to find a home again—in a future so bleak it didn't bear consideration—I would still be bereft of Bernard's love. And his love was more home than I'd ever known. I couldn't lose it now.

Mama stared at me with cold hatred. "This couldn't possibly be your sister. Astrid was a liar and a cheat. She never cared about anyone except herself. She deserved that curse, and she deserved her death."

"No one deserves to live like this," Violet said, shaking, dry heaving.

It was then that I saw one of the welts across her right ankle had opened. Red blood oozed over the rusted scab. How long had Violet been shackled like a prisoner? One year? Two?

I pressed my clean handkerchief to Violet's wound.

"Is it true?" Bernard asked me quietly. "You suffer a similar affliction? Is this why you do not speak?" He touched his rough fingers to my cheek. "Darling, no one would blame you for a moment for wishing to avoid such an appalling fate. Tell me now. Speak the words. Our love is strong enough to bear such misfortunes."

"You may feel differently when you learn my eldest spat up toads and snakes," Mama said, pouring herself another glass from the decanter.

Bernard's hand fell from my face. His other, still tangled with mine, went rigid.

"Please, Astrid. Please!" Violet begged. "Tell him who you are."

"Enough of this," Bernard said, tugging on my hand. "Lucia is mute. And you both need a different act." He dropped a few coins at Mama's feet. "Coughing up glass shards and pretending they are diamonds—really. Come away, Lucia."

"Astrid, no!" Violet said weakly.

My brow furrowed and prickled with sweat. "Wait," I whispered.

Bernard didn't hear me. He held open the tent flap. The festival streets were overrun with midday bustle and noise.

My stomach cramped, and the sickening slither began to climb up my throat. I wasn't fool enough to believe that what I was about to do would end my curse. It would end my marriage, surely.

Bernard wouldn't love me after he saw that everything Mama said was true. I was a monster, and he would be at the front of the mob running me out of town for what was about to transpire. No more bread making. No more nights spent in his arms. No more kind words or sweet smiles. I'd be left to roam the countryside without so much as a basket or spare pair of shoes—a fate I deserved. I was a cheat and a liar. Bernard loved me only because I concealed my true nature from him. He deserved better.

But so did Violet.

Mama was wrong about one thing. I cared more about Bernard and Violet than I cared about myself. I could act now and free Violet. I'd lose Bernard. I'd lose the man I loved. A man who was kind, clever, and messier than a vole in spring mud, but he'd find someone else. Someone honest and sweet who could speak her love openly. That's what he needed. More than any washed linen, mended shirts, or warm meals, that's what he needed. This would hurt, but both Bernard and Violet would be better off for it.

And to think I had earlier hoped the witch's warning had been a muddled message of glad tidings.

"Wait." I shouted it this time, even as the slithering worked its way higher into my throat.

Bernard dropped the tent flap, his lips set in a weak grimace, his eyes brimmed with pain. And fear.

Mama's face twisted in revulsion, but Violet stopped crying and looked up, beaming. Her hopeful smile breathed life back into my fragile heart.

"It's true," I said, and vomited a tangle of snakes and toads. The snakes writhed in a wet puddle. The toads hopped a few paces, sending Mama jumping onto her chair.

"She is my sister. And my name is Astrid Lucia. And..." I doubled over and was sick again. This time, a single large hooded snake landed, hissing, on the floor. "I am cursed."

"Lucia," Bernard said, squeezing his eyes tight. "Astrid Lucia." He pressed both of his hands to his eyes. "Why didn't you tell me?"

"Because"—I clutched my stomach—"I didn't want you to hate me." I retched out a fat, warty bullfrog. All the creatures were enormous now. I hadn't spoken aloud in months; maybe that's why they were bigger than usual. Or had I provoked them when I'd spoken that single word in the attic. *Love.* "People hate me. I'm a monster who vomits toads and snakes. I'm a hateful creature who breeds other hateful creatures in the most revolting way possible."

"Hush," Bernard said sternly. "I will not hear another word."

I realized then that I'd been a fool to think a monster like me could ever deserve even a sliver of happiness.

"You are well rid of her, I say," Mama said, then screeched at a little snake that slithered too close.

Bernard groaned and pressed a fist to his lips.

He was disgusted by me, and the weight of that truth was crushing. It hurt more than anything I'd ever felt in the years of being spat at.

"What will you do now, Astrid?" Mama stomped on a toad that came too near her. "I'm not going to take you in, you can be sure of that."

I needed to stay strong. Violet needed me to stay strong. "I'm going to do what I should have done three years ago. I'm taking Violet." I retched again. Lots of lizards. I grabbed one that was a brilliant orange and blue. "And if you think you can stop me," I panted and shoved the reptile close to her face, "I will tell the beasts to eat you. All of them. They listen to me." They of course didn't, but Mama didn't need to know this.

She recoiled and swatted the lizard from my hand. I should have known better. Mama was always bluster and rage. "Where will you go?" she demanded. "What town would take in a monster like you?"

"I know how to survive in the woods." I stumbled backward and coughed up a newt.

"Of course you do, mean little thing that you are. But what of Violet?"

My shoulders slumped. Violet was far too frail for a winter in the woods.

"You'll kill her if you take her and run." Mama cackled. "You've lost, Astrid. No one wants you. Even that mess of a potter that you've been lying to." Mama sneered. "I hope you didn't marry her," she said to Bernard. "She'll rob you blind. Steal all your money and your happiness and future besides."

Bernard stood there frozen, his eyes swimming in confusion and sadness. I looked away. I wouldn't look at him again. I didn't want to witness the moment when the hurt and pain on his face turned to hatred.

"But—" I gagged, but pressed on. "Violet doesn't deserve this—" My words were cut off by coughing, wheezing, and spluttering. A hard, sharp knot lodged in my throat. A turtle. Oh no. Was I to die by choking on a turtle?

"Violet has been blessed," Mama shouted over my gasps and retching, "and if her fate was so horrible and you were so concerned for her welfare, why didn't you do something about it sooner? Why did you leave? We thought you were dead." Mama ground her foot harder onto another unfortunate toad. "I wish you were dead."

My eyes bulged with such intensity I feared they might pop. I dropped to the floor. My face was hot, no doubt red, and tear-stained with the effort to breathe, and just when I feared I'd taken my last breath, I felt a small hand on the base of my neck.

"I don't," Violet said, wrapping my cloak around my shoulders.

I expelled a large yellow-dotted pond turtle.

I gasped for air on my hands and knees. "I made a mistake, Violet. I shouldn't have left. I thought you'd be better off without me, but I should never have left you. I thought it was what you wanted." I retched, but it was thankfully only frogs this time. "I'm sorry."

"I'm sorry for calling you a monster, Astrid." Violet wiped the turtle's shell dry with the hem of her dress.

I stroked her dark hair. It was thin and had lost its shine. "It's okay. I am one."

"No, you aren't!" Violet hiccupped, and a diamond tumbled to the floor. The turtle snapped at it with its little beaked snout. "Sir, tell her she's not."

I met my husband's eyes for the briefest of moments before wincing and dropping my gaze to the floor. I'd hurt him. I'd used him. I'd lied to him. I never deserved his love. I certainly didn't deserve his pity now. I didn't even deserve a goodbye.

Bernard tried to move, but the hooded snake I'd coughed up earlier was coiled, hissing, at his boot. I waited for him to kick it aside. To leave me alone and wretched for the rest of my days. He'd find someone else. Someone who wasn't a monster.

Bernard huffed and bent down to pick up the snake, holding it gently but firmly by its head while its body thrashed and curled around his arm.

"Madam," he said calmly to my mother. "It is time for you to say goodbye to your daughters. You will not be seeing them again after today."

Mama frowned. "What on earth are you talking about?"

"Violet will be coming to live with us." He helped me to my feet with his free hand.

"I see how it is," Mama said grabbing the decanter and rising to her feet. "You'd trade in the foul daughter for the blessed one, but no one has use for a disgusting woman. I couldn't even sell that one to a circus. Revolting." She threw the decanter to the floor. "I'll have to drown her in a lake."

Tears drained from my eyes. It didn't matter what I did, I was cursed. I deserved a cursed fate, but Violet didn't. "Please, Bernard. I don't care what happens to me, but you have to help Violet." I shook and retched a half-dozen pink and brown toads all over Bernard's boots.

Bernard pressed his hand gently between my shoulder blades. "But I care very much what happens to you."

He pulled me into his arms and kissed the top of my head.

I started sobbing. Bernard wasn't leaving me. He wasn't repulsed by my curse. He didn't hate me. He loved me. I couldn't believe it, but I felt it.

Mama spat on the fine carpet. "I don't know what twisted fascination you see in the wench, but she's good for nothing. Possessed of a calculating black heart."

"Madam, please," Bernard said, grabbing a throw from the settee and wrapping it around Violet's shoulders. "Your poisoned tongue has done enough damage. We are leaving, and we are taking Violet with us."

"Never. I'm warning you, Astrid has venom in her heart. She poisoned Violet against me. She will poison you. Ruin your life just as she has sought to ruin mine!"

"Enough!" He brought the snake within striking distance of Mama. It hissed and writhed against Bernard's grip. "I will put it to you in business terms." His tone became stern. "What customer would seek to buy a bauble for his beloved that came from the stomach of a poor, wretched little girl?"

Mama's eye twitched, and a vein in her forehead bulged. "You want this wealth for yourself, but it is mine."

"I want nothing more than to sit at my wheel and provide a happy, comfortable life for my wife and her sister. One where they need not speak another word if they so choose." Bernard took Violet's pail filled with stones and flowers and dumped it on the carpet. He unwound the snake from his arm and placed it gently inside, along with the bullfrog that had hopped onto the pile of flowers.

Mama shook with rage. "Astrid is a monster. A vile, conniving little monster."

"Astrid *Lucia* is my wife. Now, we will be going, and if I hear another word from you, I'll be setting this fine snake out on your table. How would your customers take to him, I wonder?" Bernard tucked the pail under his arm and offered me his elbow. "Ready, darling?"

I didn't hesitate for a moment. "As ever," I said, turning to spit one last snake out in Mama's tent.

Bernard pressed his lips into a smile. "Violet?"

Violet picked up the turtle and a single pink rose from the pile of wet flowers that left a stain on the carpet. The creature took quick, snapping bites at the petals. "Can I keep him?"

"Only if you introduce us properly," Bernard said.

"Mr. Tilly Shiny Shell."

"Pleased to meet you Mr. Tilly Shiny Shell. I am Bernard, Lucia's husband and Violet's new brother." Bernard made a slight bow as he touched his hand to the turtle's foot. "Now, Violet," he said, straightening, "you'll need a proper dress. If you see any you fancy along the way, just tug at my sleeve. All right? We'll get on with pointing and gesturing as best we can and see if that doesn't settle your stomach before luncheon. Same goes for you, my dear."

I smiled at Bernard, my lips pressed into a wide arc.

"Doesn't that sort of thoughtfulness merit a kiss?" He tapped his cheek. "One right there, I should think."

I rose on tiptoe and kissed my husband's cheek.

Bernard smiled. "Goodbye, Mother," he called. "Enjoy the festival. May we never meet again."

CHAPTER SEVEN

Thankfully, Violet quickly found a pink cloak on our way through the festival streets. Bernard was without his purse, but the merchant was more than willing to trade.

"Such a waste of wealth," the man said, inspecting Mama's throw with a quizzing glass. Like everything else in the tent, it was encrusted with gemstones. "I've never seen anything more gauche."

"I have," Bernard said, squeezing my hand.

I nearly laughed at that. Instead, my lips trembled and eyes stung with tears. The panic I'd felt at the eminent loss of everything precious was still too close for me not to feel churned up and raw inside. I was shaking, try as I might to conceal it, with a knot of emotions, an army of thoughts, a bale of sensations. I could scream for joy or dance in a blind rage. I could fall to the ground, overwhelmed by relief, or run for miles fueled on regret. It was the sort of brew that would swirl into a cyclone of self-destruction if I was left untethered.

Bernard wrapped a tender arm around my shoulders as we waited for the merchant to finish his appraisal. My husband loved me, cursed as I was, and I loved him. Violet would be safe in our home, of this I had no doubt.

The merchant dropped his quizzing glass and held the throw at arm's length as he studied it, his nose wrinkled. "I'll have to separate the gems by size and color, and even then I'll have more than I know what to do with. There's enough here to bejewel a hundred garments." He flipped the throw over and gasped. "Two hundred. I didn't realize they covered both sides."

The merchant traded us the throw for the cloak and a lidded basket, which Bernard promptly put to good use as soon as we found a quiet alley. "No sign of the bullfrog," he said with amusement. "That long fellow must have been hungry. Are we ready?"

I fastened the pink cloak around Violet's shoulders. My heart both broke and mended as she smoothed her small hands over the soft wool. She twirled twice before taking my hand and then Bernard's.

Timothy and Maria had a lot of words for us when at last we arrived at our festival stall. They immediately stopped when they saw Violet. Bernard promised to tell the whole story that night, but Maria wouldn't let it rest. When she'd gotten the whole of it, right down to the visit to the merchant, she grabbed the basket and took off.

She returned after a short while with a white wool dress, a pair of boots, silk stockings, and two matching yellow ribbons. "One for you and one for the turtle," she said, handing the ribbons to Violet, who screamed for joy. "The rest is being delivered to the bakery tomorrow."

"What?" Bernard asked.

Maria plated a pair of almond croissants for a waiting customer. "I wasn't about to let you trade a fortune in gems for a cloak and a basket."

"What did you do with the snake?" Bernard asked warily.

Maria shrugged. "I sold him."

Bernard nearly dropped the platter he was wrapping in paper. "You what?"

"To a snake charmer. Before the creature could get any ideas about the turtle, which reminds me." Maria reached into her pocket and handed Violet a silver crown.

Violet stared at the coin before pointing at the yellow-iced petits fours.

Maria smiled. She pointed to one of the yellow ribbons in Violet's hands. Violet added it to her open palm next to the coin. Maria took the ribbon and curled Violet's fingers around the coin. "Family members get all the cakes they want for free," she said, then tied the ribbon around Violet's hair.

"Turtles too," said Timothy, handing a plate with two yellow cakes on it to Violet.

We were busy selling the rest of the day. Business showed no sign of slowing as the sun set. I slipped my hand into Bernard's. He pulled me into his arms. "Oh, love. I'm so glad you came."

I smiled, but nodded with my chin toward Violet. She sat huddled in the back of the stall, shaking despite the contented smile on her face.

Bernard's mouth quirked up at one corner, but his eyes remained solemn. "Maria, Timothy. Why don't you let us finish up tonight?"

"And eat what's left of the Danishes?" Timothy called.

Bernard cleared his throat and pointed with his thumb at Violet, who was dozing off despite the cold.

Maria untied her apron and crouched in front of Violet. "I think Tilly might be getting cold. Let's take him home and give him a warm bath."

Violet nodded, holding the turtle close to her chest, wrapping him in her cloak. She wobbled to her legs, but fell down, exhausted.

"It's okay, dear. Timothy can carry you home."

"Do you want Lucia to come?" Bernard asked. He caught my gaze and smiled shyly. "I was hoping you would stay and help me sell the last of these pretty plates, but if you think Violet needs you"—he swallowed—"I'll manage."

My heart warmed. My husband wanted me to stay. With him.

Violet was already asleep in Timothy's arms. "We'll be fine," Maria said. "I'll make her a bed downstairs. A quiet night and some warm broth is all she needs. Don't worry."

CURSES, DIAMONDS, & TOADS

It was long past midnight before we found ourselves walking back to Timothy and Maria's bakery.

Bernard took my hand. "I understand why you didn't tell me," he said. "I also understand if you never wish to say another word, but I hope someday you will."

I squeezed his hand.

"I'm not a perfect man, Lucia. You know this. I'd let the chickens into the house and forget to wash for a fortnight if left to my own whims. I'm a simple potter, but I'm no fool. I'm not going to let a silly curse spoil a happy life with the woman I love." He pulled me into his arms. "And I have no interest—none—in becoming a jeweler."

I wrapped my arms tightly around Bernard's waist.

My husband kissed the top of my head. "Violet will be safe with us. She can spend the rest of her days in silence. She can be my apprentice if she wants, or while away the hours staring up at the clouds. I don't care, so long as she is safe and happy." He cupped my face. "So long as you both are safe and happy."

I kissed Bernard's cheek before kissing each of his eyes closed.

He held me tighter. "You want me to close my eyes?"

I nodded. I didn't want to chance a knot of snakes or toads spoiling what I was about to say.

"Why?" he said. "I just told you that I don't care."

Please, Bernard? my shaking smile said.

He inhaled slowly before closing his eyes. "Fine."

My stomach turned, but with sensations more fluttery than snakes or toads. I took a deep breath, not caring if the words I said cost me hours of retching. Knowing only that I wanted to speak them, had to speak them.

"Bernard," I said, "I love you." I paused and smiled though my stomach writhed. "I always will."

"Bernard was once a toad," Maria said at noon the next day. We'd sold the last of our wares that morning and had returned to their home, happy but exhausted.

"I was," Bernard said, beaming. "For a whole day. Never had more fun."

"Tell them what you said to the witch after she turned you back into a boy." Maria slid a new basket across the table to me.

Bernard scratched the back of his head, "Let's see. The old woman said, 'Now, then. Have you learned your lesson?' And I believe my response was, 'Can I be a snake next?'"

We all laughed, and laughter, I was discovering, rarely triggered my curse.

Maria ruffled Bernard's hair. "He's been fascinated by the beasties ever since."

Timothy sat with his arms crossed, staring at the basket of toads I had coughed up when Bernard and I had told them the details of our courtship. Bernard, thankfully, had done most of the talking.

"I'm not sure I understand," Timothy said. "You"—he pointed at me—"have been with him"—he pointed at Bernard—"since last spring. And you hadn't said a single word?"

I nodded.

"That's right," Bernard said.

"How? I've had to tell him at least twice every quarter hour to wash his hands before touching my pastries. The man tracks mud everywhere he goes."

I laughed heartily. "I had a lot to say in the woods every night, believe me." I cleared my throat, coughed, and when I cleared it again, a snake slithered out of my mouth and darted onto the table.

"I got it," Maria said, catching the striped creature in the empty basket.

Bernard groaned and put his hands to his eyes.

I tried not to blush. I knew Bernard wasn't repulsed by me, but that didn't change the fact that my curse was...unnatural.

"What's the matter, brother?" Timothy demanded. "Too much sugar upsetting your stomach? I warned you not to eat the rest of the Danishes."

Bernard dropped his hands, "Of course not. I was thinking about all the nights I've made Lucia suffer for my silly pots and plates. It's shameful. When I think of it... I was no better than your horrid mother."

"No!" I placed my hand on top of Bernard's and squeezed. He was *nothing* like Mama.

"I don't think that's fair, Bernard," Marie said. "It was Lucia's choice to provide you with the creatures, and she did so in the manner of her choosing."

"That's right," I said, then heaved up dozens of thimble-sized frogs into the basket. "Violet had no choice." Mama made sure of that. "But I did." I heaved again and spat out a small pink lizard. "I chose you."

Bernard threaded his fingers through my own and brought my hand to his lips. "If I'd known, I never would have asked for the beasties." He slid a hand to the base of my neck. "Is the nausea returning?"

I pressed my arm against my stomach and nodded, surprised that it'd taken this long for it to catch up to me. Maybe the curse was weakening?

"And Violet's curse has the same effect?" Timothy said, stroking his beard. "Sickness and nausea accompany her words?"

"The same." Bernard said. "Worse, perhaps. Because what dredges up from her stomach is of value to everyone, not just inventive potters." He kissed my shoulder.

"These curses must be undone," Maria said.

Yes, but how? I rose to check on Violet. She lay wrapped among the blankets and straw we'd used to transport Bernard's earthenware and ceramics. Maria and Bernard had built a nest for the turtle out of a small wooden crate. It lay in the corner of the straw bed. Violet had fallen asleep with her hand over it. She was small and far too thin for an eleven-year-old, but her color had improved tremendously since yesterday.

"It's not safe to live with such a curse." Maria rose to refill everyone's teacups. "One woman without words won't draw suspicion, but two in a village will."

"What is to be done?" Timothy asked.

Bernard crossed his arms at his chest. "We have to find a witch."

Maria scoffed. "Not before Violet's strength returns."

"Aye," Timothy agreed. "The journey home will be ordeal enough for the little thing."

"And there's the turtle to think of," Maria added.

"Enough," Bernard said, throwing his hands in the air. "I will amend my statement. We have to find a witch after Violet has convalesced, the turtle is comfortable, and the weather is fair. Then, and only then, will we begin our witch-hunt. Now, does anyone know where we might start?"

"I do," I said, before spitting out a toad.

CHAPTER EIGHT

We didn't have to borrow a mule for the journey home. We'd bought one from the merchant who'd traded us for Mama's bejeweled throw. "Take anything," the man said, refusing our gold. "Just tell your sister to keep that cobra away from my shop."

We traveled for days, past snowy fields and leafless trees. New boots and cloaks made the journey home easy, but we stopped at warm inns whenever Violet started shaking or the skies clouded over. Days turned into weeks before we were back at Bernard's house. Our home.

Violet's appetite improved, but she was more tired than I ever remembered her being. She spent most of that winter sleeping. And when she wasn't sleeping, she was eating or making bonnets for the turtle.

We waited until spring to make the journey up the mountain. Mud made our progress even slower than it had been for me in late summer. Violet was fast asleep in Bernard's arms when at last we knocked on Gertrude's door.

"Good mother," I called, "we seek your wisdom."

The witch opened the door, a pipe in her hand. She squinted at me then at Bernard and Violet. "You're late."

"The spring mud," I said, turning to cough up a toad.

"Leave your boots by the door." Gertrude ushered us inside. "Put the little one there on the bed. Mind the cats. They refused to venture out this evening. Would have saved me considerable trouble if you'd been on time."

Bernard laid sleeping Violet on the bed. "We seek a cure, dear mother. For both Violet here and my wife, Lucia."

"They have the cure. What they want is to speed the recovery." Gertrude poked the embers of her fire. "Something to manage the symptoms while the magic grows roots in their hearts." She added a log to the flames. "Remedies are all I can offer."

"But—" Bernard began, but I clapped my hand over his mouth. Best not to argue with a witch.

Bernard kissed my palm before removing my hand.

"The little one's is simple enough." Gertrude shuffled around her cottage. "She must swallow a toad each night from tomorrow's full moon until the next. Now, the tricky part"—Gertrude paused to open a cupboard—"is keeping the toad down. Toads don't like to stay down. You can ask Astrid Lucia about this." She rummaged among the shelves, pulling out several vials and jars. "They climb back up. Nasty business to have even a frog in the throat, but imagine a toad. Oh." She closed the cupboard door. "Even worse."

The larger tomcat wove around the witch's feet, purring ferociously. "Fortunately, Old Gertrude is clever. I boiled, dried, and pulverized the toads your wife brought me when she was here last. Set them in capsules. See?" She rattled a glass jar filled with grayish-green pills in Bernard's face before setting it on the table. "Thirty toads. All sorted and ready for you."

"And what of my curse, Gertrude?" I pressed a hand to my stomach and breathed through the writhing.

"That remedy is much more challenging to procure and beyond the powers of a simple witch to conjure." Gertrude shuffled to her rocking chair. "There's nothing here in my cottage to help you."

My shoulders slumped. Of course it would be this way. I rested my head in my hand.

The witch settled into her rocking chair and lit her pipe. "You look much hardier than you were last summer, Astrid Lucia. I take it the nausea has subsided?"

"To a degree, yes." Some days, it was just a deep cough that rattled my frame and brought up the beasts when I spoke. On my best days, I could speak an entire sentence, sometimes two, without triggering my curse.

"More so for Violet, I think," Bernard said. This was true. Her retching had all but stopped, and it had been weeks since she'd heaved up any flowers. A wet cough and caches of diamonds were what ailed her now. Still dangerous, but in the safety of our home, her curse was nothing more than a nuisance.

The tomcat jumped into the witch's lap. "Love works wonders on curses." Gertrude scratched the feline's chin. "I told you as much when you came last."

I frowned. "Is that it, then? Is love the cure?"

"Of course it is." The witch smiled. "Love of kin, naturally. Love of a mate, surely. But love of self, most importantly." She beckoned me close. "Could it be the latter that is impeding your progress?"

I didn't know what to say, but I did know that since I'd last visited the witch, I'd gained the love of a good man and a sister. I cherished their love, but I cherished my love for them even more. They were my home and my joy. Through their eyes, I saw I was no monster. It was enough for me. And yet...

The witch patted my hand. "These things take time—sometimes entire lifetimes—to work themselves out."

Perhaps this was true, but it was not good enough. "Gertrude, my patience has run out when it comes to this curse." I spat a small toad into my handkerchief. "I appreciate that unraveling shame and embracing compassion takes time, but I see no point in suffering any further." I fully expected to expel a knot of toads, but no beasts accompanied my words. "Please tell me the remedy. We'll find it."

"Yes, the remedy!" Bernard said, smiling broadly. "There must be something we can do."

Gertrude sucked on her pipe. "It requires the accursed to swallow a diamond, freely bought and freely given, each night of one full moon to the next." She ran a single hand down the arched back of her cat. "Difficult—very difficult—to find even one such diamond, but thirty... A fool's errand to be sure." The witch pressed her wrinkled lips into a smug smile.

"Are you serious?" I laughed. It was so easy.

"Well, when does anyone ever find a diamond they can swallow without paying for it first?"

"Daily, at our house," Bernard said. "I step on a half dozen whenever I'm in my studio. I'll have to start wearing shoes—*shoes*—if this remedy doesn't take."

"Violet is fond of talking," I said, wincing as my stomach cramped. "Particularly to her pet turtle."

The toad in my handkerchief croaked as it sprang to the floor. The cat bounded off of the witch's lap, pouncing after it, but the creature hopped under the stove out of reach.

"Interesting." The witch took the pipe from her teeth. "That you both have an abundance of everything you need."

"Gertrude, did you know all of this last summer?"

"What? That you would save each other and unravel the other's curse?" She smiled. "Swallowing diamonds works as a remedy only when they are as precious to a soul as a dead toad. If greed or self-preservation had spurred you to seek your sister, then her diamonds may have acquired the wrong sort of value and become useless. But who's to say? Love is a stronger magic in this world than any fairy's curse, more powerful and mysterious than any alchemy I wield. If love had even a foothold in your heart, I'm sure things would have turned out right in the end." Gertrude rose. "The remedies work best if taken at the same time under the same roof. Try as best you can to keep the little one from coughing an hour or two after she swallows a capsule, but don't fret if the gems bubble up." The witch took the pipe from her teeth, taping the ashes over the fire. "I added in a few extra toads for good measure."

"What about payment?" I asked, reaching for my purse.

Gertrude's impressive eyebrows bounced above her eyes. "Oh... Well, if I have a say in the matter. On market day, I want my pick of this young man's wares—"

"Done!" Bernard said.

"—for the rest of my days."

Bernard stashed the jar of green pills into the pocket of his coat. "A hard but fair bargain. Thank you, mother witch."

"I could use a new pipe. Best get to work." The witch unlatched her cottage door. The cats bolted outside. "I've never been fond of diamonds, all that sparkle without any soul, but I would fancy a little clay toad on the rim of the pipe's bowl, maybe a snake on the stem."

"I'll see to it," Bernard said, collecting Violet.

"Mind you do, or I'll turn you back into a toad."

Bernard's eyes sparkled even in the dark night.

"He should be so lucky," I said before coughing up a salamander.

"Lucia," Bernard said weeks later, after I'd swallowed my last diamond. "If I were a toad, you would still love me?"

"Completely." I kissed his lips before I returned to my work of packing Bernard's wares for market.

"And if I was never more than a messy potter?"

I frowned, my hands full of straw. "You think I fell in love with you because I had no other choice?" I packed the straw tightly into the corners of the crate.

"I think I got very, very lucky." Bernard bent over and picked up a small corn snake curled in the corner of the studio. He opened a window and freed the beast into the flower boxes that were once more filled with pink geraniums.

I dusted my hands clean and joined Bernard at the window. "And I think I might need to spend many summer nights for the rest of my days telling you all the reasons I love my kind, clever, handsome husband."

"Why only at night?" Bernard took me in his arms and kissed me. "Come with me to market tomorrow. Gertrude would love to see you, and I want to spend the day with you. Please, Lucia. Violet can come along, introduce Tilly to some new friends, buy him a new ribbon. She hasn't coughed up a gem in weeks. I know because I haven't stepped on one."

"That's a mercy." I'd never thought a potter would run out of jars, but I had begun to worry before the remedies had started to dry up the last of our curses. "Why are you smiling like that?"

"I love hearing your voice. I thought our conversations were feasts before, but now I know they were just crumbs. Please, Lucia. Come with me to market."

The crisp evening spring air tickled my face. "Things will never be the same if I do."

Bernard quirked an eyebrow. "Tell me."

"Well..." I rested my hands on his chest. "You'll sell more and at better prices. I'll make sure of that."

"I only struck bargains so I could rush home to you."

I laughed and laid my head against his chest. "I'll want to shop. You might come home with emptier pockets than when you left."

"We have a cellar full of Violet's diamonds. Enough for her to keep Tilly in the most fashionable of bonnets for a thousand years. I'm sure she'd part with some of them if we got in a pinch."

Given how in demand Bernard's pottery was, I doubted pinches were even possible. "I might buy a shop." The words thrilled me, as did the lack of any accompanying internal twists or slithers. "Someplace to keep you warm and dry on market days."

Bernard considered. "I do like staying warm."

I kissed his cheek before returning to my work of packing his ceramics. "I most assuredly will find a place for you to store your goods."

"They tend to pile up by week's end, don't they?" Bernard lifted the crates I'd packed earlier off the table and stacked them by the door.

"You'll want to wander." I considered the mountain of platters before me. Bernard had patterned them after Tilly's shell. I set the prettiest aside for our table and packed the rest. "With me there, you'll have time to do it before all the best goods are sold."

"Not the best goods, but surely the most popular." Bernard's expression turned thoughtful. "The best goods are often overlooked, appreciated only by mischievous little boys and handsome potters."

I laughed. "I'd find you a proper apprentice or two. Violet is more interested in chelonian millinery than she is in ceramics."

"She might be interested in being our shopgirl for a season. Especially if Tilly has dedicated space in the shop."

The turtle was as big as a rooster now and more fond of fancy cakes than ever. "People will come for miles just to have tea with the pair of them."

"I'll have to make more turtle-sized tea sets." Bernard joined me, packing the platters in layers of straw.

"We'll have to work something out with Timothy and Maria, start selling their petits fours." Maybe we'd be able to persuade them to open a second bakery in our village.

"They'd surely like an excuse to see Violet more often." Bernard stroked his beard. "We'll have to make arrangements with a few lace mongers. Turtles and articulate young ladies need lace at their tea tables if petits fours are on the menu."

I laughed. "Gloves too."

"Would a turtle wear lace gloves for tea?" Bernard asked.

"Does it matter if we get to watch Violet scream for joy when she sees them?"

"No." He chuckled. "Not at all."

Just then, Violet raced into the shop. "Have you seen Tilly?" she asked. "We're playing hide-and-seek, and I looked in the garden next to the strawberries, but as he ate them all yesterday, he's not there, and he's not snuggled in the chicken coop, and he's not pretending to be a rock by the back door or a statue of Adonis at the front."

"And you want us to tell you where he is?" I asked. "The last time we did that, Tilly didn't speak to us for a week."

Bernard cleared his throat and gestured to the lumps of clay on the floor near his wheel. Among them was a sleeping turtle.

"Found you!" Violet beamed, kneeling down to lay a gentle hand on the turtle's shell. "Oh, what a clever turtle you are." Violet affected a slow, deep voice with a hint of a lisp. "'And so handsome.'"

"Yes, the handsomest turtle we know, Tilly," I said before I could be accused of foul play.

"Violet?" Bernard said. "Would you like to come with us to market tomorrow? Lucia and I are looking to buy a shop."

"What sort of shop?" Violet said, swinging open a window and picking a clump of geraniums from the box.

I shook my head, knowing there was no backing out of going to market day now. "Something bright with lots of windows for all of Bernard's pretty ceramics."

"Lots of windows means lots of boxes with lots more geraniums, Tilly," Violet whispered to the turtle. Her brows drew together, and she was quiet for a moment. "Good point. I'll ask. How big of a shop?"

"Not big. Cozy." I smiled. "With just enough room to host tea parties for both people and turtles."

"You and Tilly could be our shopgirls." Bernard lifted the last crate off the table and added it to the stack. "If you like."

"I think that would be marvelous, but what say you, Mr. Shiny Shell?"

"'Oh,'" Violet drawled as she fed the geranium to the turtle, "'I think that would be cracking. Especially if it means a frilly apron. I do so love ruffles and frills.'"

"That reminds me," Violet said, scratching the turtle's neck. "Can we buy some new ribbons at market tomorrow? Tilly has grown out of his favorite dress again. I'm making him a new one, but I don't have enough pink ribbon for the sash."

"Of course," Bernard said. "In fact, Lucia needs to befriend the lace makers. Maybe you'll find some lace too."

"Oh, Tilly! You'll be the prettiest turtle in the world with lace on your new dress." Violet picked up the turtle. "Off to bed now. Growing turtles need lots of rest before busy market days. And you'll have to pick out which hat to wear." Violet spoke for Tilly again. "'But there are so many to choose from. Maybe I could wear two?'" The two of them disappeared up the stairs.

"I think," Bernard said, catching my hand, "we should follow suit. You have a busy day tomorrow. Chatting up the locals, looking at shops, spending the rest of the day by my side."

"Bernard, if I come with you to market..."

"What, love?"

"You might tire of me."

"Impossible!"

"Really? When I insist you visit the barber, fuss at you for ripping your cuffs, cosset you in front of the other tradesmen, spend a fortune on a turtle's extravagant wardrobe, tell you exactly who you should hire as your new apprentice, and inform all your customers that your prices have increased, and no, we will not be making deliveries, because we have a shop to run and tea parties to attend and—"

Bernard's eyes sparkled.

I wrapped my arms around his shoulders and kissed him. "And a lifetime of love and happiness ahead of us."

"Love, I'm counting on it."

"Good." I pulled my husband up the stairs to our bedroom. "Because I'd come for nothing less."

ACKNOWLEDGMENTS

I began writing Astrid Lucia's story after returning home from our summer trip to Austria and Switzerland. The genesis of that trip started years ago because my sister, Ona, made not one but two trips abroad possible for me. Travel is life-changing, and I am so grateful, Ona, that you thought my life was worth changing. You say that the best parts of travel often happen when you're back home. It's true. This novella is me trying to capture the best parts of my trip this summer. It was a once-in-a-lifetime experience that required the enthusiastic buy-in of every member of Team Trent, and that wouldn't have ever happened without you. We've talked about how much we've changed because of these experiences. We've talked about the resources that go into making them happen. They keep paying dividends. I saw Bernard Palissy's work seven years ago because of you. I saw the most gorgeous geraniums in every window box in Switzerland this summer because you gave us the road maps for how to do this as a family. All of my best and favorite bits of travel, especially the "rediscovery of home," as you say, became part of this novella. And yeah, it's definitely a case of "through a glass darkly," of course, but still, I'm so grateful. I thought of you when I was writing. I thought you might appreciate Astrid Lucia's pragmatism as much as I do, but if you don't, it is okay. We've got lots more world to see, so I'll just try again. Love you forever. I'm so stinkin' proud to be your sister. You and yours are some of the most amazing, smart people on this planet, and I'm so lucky to be part of your team.

This novella is an acknowledgment of my love of summer and travel as much as it is of everything else that readers have come to expect from my brand—fairy tales, romantasy, escape, comfort, whimsy, and happily ever afters. I've wanted to write a novella for a while, but I didn't know about this fairy tale, "Diamonds and Toads," until Kate Wolford, editor of *The Fairy Tale Magazine*, mentioned it in her February newsletter to the Fairy Godparents Club. Forever grateful to you, Kate! Thank you for championing lesser-known fairy tales, and thank you for publishing the writers who love them!

There are only so many places an author can sneak in actual love letters to her special someponies, and this is one of them. To Mr. Trent, I love you. I'm so proud of you, and while grapefruit stands in Portugal aren't exactly my dream, a long, loving HEA with you, wherever that may be, is.

To my daughter, wow: TS for one birthday. Switzerland for the next. And every year taller, more beautiful, more insightful, more amazing, and more you. *Je t'aime et je suis si fier de toi.* I'm not sure what next year holds, but I'm so excited I get to be a part of it. Thanks for an amazing summer, honey.

To my son, who has taught me new perspectives and refuses to settle for anything less than what is right. I love you. I am so very proud of you, and I'm still working on the dragon book. Thanks for being my buddy when we visited the open-air museum in Brienz. Do you remember the chickens outside the potter's house? I do, but only because of how they made you smile. I wrote parts of this story at the library when you were at Pokémon Club. I thought of your determination and grit in the final act when Lucia has to do hard things. I know this isn't your type of story, but our summer definitely made this novella possible. Thanks, honey.

I wanted to thank the members of my critique group, the Make-Believers. Thank you, Cindy, Arianne, Carrie, Julia, KaTrina, Georgia, Dusty, Cheree, and Ashley. Thank you, friends, for your kindness and insights. I've grown

CURSES, DIAMONDS, & TOADS

so much this past year and will cherish our Friday morning meetings forever and always.

Thank you to my editor, Joyce Lamb. You are amazing! Thank you to Sarah Rosenbarker for proofreading. You are a rock star! Kirby forever! Thank you to my aunt, Grace Burrowes, for your ongoing mentorship, publishing support, ISBNs, and love. Thank you to the V&A and the work they do in preserving the masterpieces of artists like Bernard Palissy. Thank you to the Ballenberg, Swiss Open-Air Museum for expanding my understanding of what everyday life looked like once upon a time. Thank you to my cat, Aspen, for being my little furry buddy and sometimes the only good reason any of us have for crossing the Atlantic and coming home.

One last thank you to all my readers. Thank you for reading and for bringing my characters to life in your imaginations. Thank you for subscribing to my newsletter. Writing is sometimes lonely, and having bookish friends to email monthly about the process, the joys, the comforts, and my cookie habit is amazing. Thank you for the kind reviews, recommendations, and friendship. Thank you for inviting me into your conversations, book clubs, and inboxes. Escaping into a good book is one of the greatest joys of my life, but getting a chance to talk books with friends is even better!

ALSO BY AMY TRENT

In the mood for a novel-sized romantasy?

Smoke, Steel, & Ivy is a reimaging of the classic fairy tale, The Twelve Dancing Princesses. Perfect for readers who enjoy a little adventure on their way to happily-ever-after and a smoldering romance without explicit content.

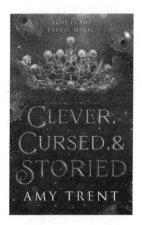

Maybe an award-winning, cozy romantasy retelling of the fairy tale, Kate Crackernuts, is more your speed? Check out *Clever, Cursed, & Storied*. Lots of banter and swoon in this one. I believe in stand-alone stories, so please know that my books can be enjoyed in any order.

Perhaps a more contemporary escape is what you need? In that case, check out my hidden-identity, sweet rom-com, *My Cosplay Escape*. Excerpts of all of these novels can be found on my website, amytrent.com. While you're there, please consider subscribing to my newsletter if you haven't done so already. I send them out monthly with info about my latest projects, giveaways, sweet escapes, and more. Hope to see you there!

XO,

Amy

Made in the USA
Coppell, TX
27 December 2024

43597608R00048